The $66 Summer

The $66 Summer

John Armistead

Illustrated by Fran Gregory

MILKWEED EDITIONS

Published 2000 by Milkweed Editions
Printed in the United States of America
Cover design by Sarah Purdy
Cover painting and interior illustrations by Fran Gregory
Author photo by Lisa Roberts
Interior design by Wendy Holdman
The text of this book is set in Charlotte Book.
00   01   02   03   04   5   4   3   2   1
First Edition

Milkweed Editions, a nonprofit publisher, gratefully acknowledges support for our intermediate fiction from Alliance for Reading funders: Silicon Graphics, Inc.; Dayton Hudson Project Imagine; Ecolab Foundation; Gannet Foundation/Kare 11; Musser Fund; Jay and Rose Phillips Foundation; Target Stores; United Arts Partnership Funds. Other support has been provided by Elmer L. and Eleanor J. Andersen Foundation; James Ford Bell Foundation; Bush Foundation; Dayton Hudson Foundation on behalf of Dayton's, Mervyn's California and Target Stores; General Mills Foundation; Honeywell Foundation; Jerome Foundation; McKnight Foundation; Minnesota State Arts Board through an appropriation by the Minnesota State Legislature; Norwest Foundation on behalf of Norwest Bank Minnesota; Oswald Family Foundation; Ritz Foundation on behalf of Mr. and Mrs. E. J. Phelps Jr.; John and Beverly Rollwagen Fund of the Minneapolis Foundation; St. Paul Companies, Inc.; Star Tribune Foundation; U.S. Bancorp Piper Jaffray Foundation on behalf of U.S. Bancorp Piper Jaffray; and generous individuals.

Library of Congress Cataloging-in-Publication Data

Armistead, John.
    The $66 summer / John Armistead.
      p.   cm.
    Summary: While working in his grandmother's store in Obadiah, Alabama, during the summer of 1955, thirteen-year-old George becomes friends with two Black children with whom he stumbles onto evidence of a violent death.
     ISBN 1-57131-626-4 — ISBN 1-57131-625-6 (pbk.)
     [1. Prejudices—Fiction. 2. Friendship—Fiction. 3. Afro-Americans—Fiction. 4. Race relations—Fiction. 5. Grandmothers—Fiction.] I. Title: Sixty-six dollar summer. II. Title.

PZ7.A728 Aae 2000
[Fic]—dc21   99-045464

This book is printed on acid-free paper.

For my granddaughter,
Charlotte

The only reward of virtue is virtue;
the only way to have a friend is to be one.

Ralph Waldo Emerson (1803 – 1882)

The $66 Summer

One

My mother always told me my father was a liar, but I didn't believe her until that day when I found out he had lied about telling me the truth. I think he thought he was saving me from a lot of trouble, maybe even from getting murdered. But his lying killed something deeper within me than life itself.

It all began on a Saturday in 1955 just after school let out for the summer. He almost got me killed on that day, too.

"Wake up, George," Daddy said, shaking my shoulder. His mouth was against my ear, and he was talking very softly, I knew, so as not to awaken Tony, my little brother, who was sleeping on the bottom bunk. "We're leaving in ten minutes."

I groaned and rolled over away from him. I felt like I'd just gone to sleep.

"Come on," he said, shaking harder and pulling back the covers.

We were going fishing in Mobile Bay just off Cedar Point as we did almost every Saturday morning. As far as Daddy was concerned, you couldn't leave too early to go fishing. All week long, he said, as he painted the clapboard military buildings at Brookley Field, he thought about getting out in the boat on Saturday morning.

It was still dark when we left the house. The streets were wet with rain and shone in the car's headlights. As we turned onto Government Street, I lay my head back on the seat and closed my eyes. I wished I were still in bed sleeping for another couple of hours. Then I could go over to Sam's.

It's not that I didn't like to fish. I did, but on Thursday my friend Sam Jeffreys had gotten a Cushman Highlander motor scooter. His father ran a filling station, and he'd taken the scooter in on trade for some work he'd done on a man's car, and Sam was buying it from him for sixty-five dollars.

When Sam got off work last night, he stopped by my house, and I hopped on back of his motor scooter and we rode out beyond Springhill College and back. And that's why I hadn't been able to sleep. All night long I kept thinking how much I wanted a motor scooter—maybe a Cushman Eagle or a Vespa. I tossed and turned and wondered what Daddy and Mama would say.

Probably that I was too young. But I'd be thirteen in two weeks, I could argue, and Sam was only thirteen, just four months older than me.

All through the night I rehearsed over and over again how I would mention getting a motor scooter to Daddy. The fishing trip would be an ideal time to bring it up. Daddy would be at his mellowest.

I was jolted out of my thoughts when the car stopped. Daddy had parked in front of Johnny's, the all-night diner just beyond the Loop, the place where we usually had breakfast.

We sat on the stools at the counter. Except for two men at a table beside the window, there were no other customers.

The waitress was new. She had black hair and smiled big as she handed each of us a breakfast menu covered with yellowed plastic. "Going fishing, I bet," she said, setting a glass of ice water in front of me.

"Yes, ma'am," I replied.

"Ma'am?" she said with a teasing smile.

I looked up at her, confused.

"Eggs and grits," Daddy said. There was a hardness in his tone. "And coffee. For both of us."

"Yes, *sir*," she said, placing a glass of water in front of him. She turned and called out the order to the cook.

I glanced at Daddy. His jaw was clamped tight, and his cheek muscle was twitching like it always did when he was upset. I couldn't imagine what was bothering him all of a sudden.

Afterward, we got into the car, and Daddy spun tires in the gravel as he steered back onto the road. "Uppity high yellow," he said through his teeth. "She was making fun of you for saying ma'am to her."

"Sir?"

"She was colored."

"She looked white."

"But she was colored," he repeated. His cheek was beginning to twitch again.

He drove faster. Daddy always drove fast when he got upset.

I didn't want him upset. I wanted to talk about my motor scooter. "Why did you sell your motorcycle?" I asked.

Until two years ago, Daddy had owned a 1948 Harley-Davidson. Dark blue.

"A man wanted it more than I did," he said. "The thing is, son, President Eisenhower and the Supreme Court may think they can just run all over us about this colored thing, but they're going to find out that the people in the South won't stand for it. It's not our way. It's not God's way."

"Grandma says Elizabeth is her best friend," I said, and I knew immediately I should have kept my mouth shut. I didn't need to get into it again with him right now. I needed to let him calm down.

He gave a snort. "Your grandmother is a bit fluffy in the head. But believe me, there are still certain lines that Elizabeth won't cross. She knows her place."

Elizabeth had been working for Grandma for years, and she really was Grandma's best friend, just like her son Bennett was my best friend whenever I was in Obadiah, which was a lot—Christmas and Easter and several weeks each summer.

"They just aren't responsible like white people," Daddy continued. He was driving faster now. "Take that Staple running off like that."

Staple was Elizabeth's husband and the father of Bennett, Esther, and Winston. He'd disappeared a few years ago, and Mama said the reason Daddy talked so hard about it was because his own father had run off when Daddy was only six.

He was really driving fast now. I wished he'd slow down. I wanted to get his mind on motorcycles. I said, "I like Sam's motor scooter. We went riding on it last night."

But Daddy didn't reply. We drove the rest of the way to Cedar Point in silence.

He pulled into the white shell-paved parking lot beside the bait shop and went inside to buy a carton of shrimp and rent the boat.

I turned to face the bay. The flat water now glowed orange as the rising sun fell over it. I smelled the pungent odor of sulfur from the low tide. Seagulls swooped up and down along the pier where several old men and women were already crabbing.

I looked out toward Dauphin Island. Beyond the island was the Gulf of Mexico, and immediately I felt a longing to get away from Mobile, Alabama, to join the merchant marines someday and sail to distant places.

"We're in number nine," Daddy said when he came out. He was carrying a pair of oars on his shoulder and the carton of shrimp in his hand.

The man who ran the bait shop followed him. He was skinny and bald and had a wrinkled face. He smiled at me with brown teeth. "Should be a good day," he said. "Just watch those clouds. You know how fast something can build up. Had a man get knocked over and drown last summer when one of those quick squalls hit."

We untied the rods and reels from the rack on top of the car, unloaded the rest of the gear from the trunk, and took it all down to the line of rowboats pulled up onto a bank of dirty sand. Daddy carried the rods and the tin tackle box, and I carried the cardboard box that contained our lunch and two thermos bottles. The old man gave us a hand sliding the boat down into the water.

I stepped into the boat and moved to the stern seat as Daddy pushed us off. He settled himself in the middle seat, slid each oar into a lock, and began rowing with long easy strokes out toward the island.

I reached into the cardboard box between us and picked up the red thermos. The red thermos was for me. Coffee with lots of milk and a generous portion of sugar. The dark blue thermos was for Daddy. It was filled with whiskey.

"It's all right," he said.

I was pouring coffee into the cup. I looked up at him. "Sir?"

"I got fooled myself once. I was on the bus going

down Dauphin Street to town. The bus was full, and this woman got on and started up the aisle. I stood up to offer her my seat, but she kept right on walking all the way to the back. Did I feel like an idiot. She looked as white as any white woman you ever seen."

He slipped the oars and took his pipe out of his shirt pocket and a can of Prince Albert from his trouser pocket. After he lit the pipe, he puffed and said, "It could happen to anybody." He began rowing again.

There were three other boats between us and the island. One was a bigger boat with a cabin, and the other two were rowboats.

"Do you think you'll ever buy another motorcycle?" I asked.

"Never can tell," he said. He slipped the oars again and reached for the blue thermos. "But even if one of them is as light as that woman at the diner, the blood is always there. It's colored blood, and it'll show up. I mean, she could marry a white man who didn't know any better, maybe a Yankee, and she could have a child as black as the ace of spades."

He poured his cup half full and put the cork back into the thermos. "We'll try here awhile," he said. "This is where we caught that mess last time. Where'd you put the shrimp?"

I knew as the morning wore on, he would get more relaxed. He always did. I was counting on it. Of course, what I hadn't counted on was the way he'd gotten upset at the diner. I needed to let his anger wear off a bit, and then I could ask him about my motor scooter.

Midmorning, he opened two cans of Vienna sausage and a package of crackers. We ate, and I drank from my thermos and he drank from his. We had moved to another spot, farther out, still in the direction of the island.

"Sam is paying only sixty-five dollars for his Highlander," I said.

He didn't reply. He was staring out toward the water. I had no idea where his mind was.

I took a deep breath, then blurted out, "I thought I'd get a job this summer and save up to buy me one."

He took a long drink from his cup and refilled it. He drank again and looked at me, his eyes squinting. "What's that?"

"I said I thought I'd get a job this summer and save up to buy a motor scooter like Sam's. Only I'd rather have a Cushman Eagle."

He looked back toward the other side of the bay and slowly nodded. "I don't know about those Cushmans," he said. "What you ought to look for is one of those little Harleys." He drank again, wiped his mouth with the back of his hand, and picked up his pipe. "It's just a one cylinder, of course. But I rode one once. It had good snap to it."

I couldn't believe what he'd just said. He had, in effect, said it was okay for me to buy a motorcycle.

"Yes," I said, hardly breathing. "I think that would be good."

The wind was picking up, and the water was getting choppy. I noticed thick dark clouds were coming quickly from the west.

He pulled out his tobacco can again, fumbled with it and dropped it to the floor of the boat, snatched it up, and refilled the pipe bowl. "First of all," he said, "you need to get a job." He lit the pipe, puffed, and tossed the match into the water. "That's just the trouble with coloreds. They don't really want to work."

The waves were rising now, and I thought about what the old man at the bait shop had said.

"No, they just want to laze around," Daddy continued. "They're all right as long as they remember their place. But you have to watch them, or they'll get out of line." He took another drink and gave a wry smile. "I had a friend once who caught one in back of his house drinking from the dipper at the well."

"Looks like a strong blow moving in," I said, looking toward the other boats. The two rowboats were already moving closer to the shoreline. It was beginning to rain.

The waves were surging higher now, lifting the bow of the boat and dropping it back into the water with thudding flops. Daddy was still smiling at me and nodding his head.

"I'm talking about the very dipper the whole family used," he continued. A large wave broke over the side and drenched us both. Daddy pitched to one side and grabbed the gunnel for support. "Well, that was the wrong thing to do," he said over the wind. "Made my friend furious."

It was suddenly as dark as night. Both thermoses crashed together on the deck between us. I turned my face from the lash of the rain.

"Listen," Daddy yelled, standing up and swaying back and forth. "He shot and killed him. I mean, killed him right then and there."

The boat pitched up high on the starboard side, and another wave thundered over us. I grabbed onto the side of the boat and closed my eyes for a moment.

I shuddered and looked around.

Daddy was gone.

"Daddy!" I yelled, jumping up.

The boat shot up straight in the air, and something whammed into the back of my head and I was in the water, sinking and thrashing out with my hands and arms, trying to grab the boat, but the force of the water hurled me down, farther and farther.

Two

Everything was black and I was upside down and the force of the water twisted my head one way and my body another way. The water was cold and I jabbed out my hands as the water spun me over and over. I thought I was about to crash to the bottom of the bay. Suddenly the water became warm and my head burst through the surface. I gasped for a breath and was sucked under again.

My arms fought to the surface once more, and I heard someone shout. I went under for a moment, then popped up again.

"There!" came another shout. "There's one!"

My eyes stung from the salt water, and I tried to see but couldn't.

"Grab the line!" someone yelled.

I was still turning my head and dog-paddling. Now I could hear the engine of a motor above the roar of the wind.

My hand touched a rope, a line, and I grabbed it. At once it ran fast through my hands, as if someone were snatching it away. A hard cork life preserver crashed against the side of my head. Someone had thrown it beyond me and pulled it back. I grabbed and held on with all my might.

The life preserver, with me on top, was jerked through the water. Waves smashed over me again and again, and I felt hands seize me and haul me out of the water.

I was laid on my back. My vision was blurred, but I could see several faces looking down at me.

"Daddy—" I gasped, then coughed.

Someone put a hand on my shoulder. "Easy now, son," he said. "You're all right."

I pulled myself to a sitting position and knew I had to be on the larger fishing boat that I'd seen out from us toward the island. Across the deck sitting on the floor with his hands on his knees was Daddy. He gave me a weak smile and nodded his head.

Even before we reached the shore, the wind had slackened and the waves ceased pitching so bad. We rode the swells closer and closer to the bait shop's pier. The rain had stopped, and the sky seemed to be lightening up as quickly as it had turned dark.

There were four men on the fishing boat. They made fast against the pier and helped Daddy and me out. The old man who ran the bait shop hurried outside. His eyes were wide and he shouted, "Where's my boat?"

Daddy pushed him aside. "Your boat!" he said, stumbling toward the parking lot. "What about my gear? We almost drowned out there. You should be arrested for renting a boat like that. That's a boat for a pond, not for the bay."

"Where do you think you're going?" the man said, following Daddy. "You're responsible for my boat."

Daddy opened the car door, got in, and slammed the door shut, almost getting the man's fingers. I scrambled onto the passenger seat.

The man was screaming something at us as we drove away.

I began to shake with a chill and folded my arms across my chest. My eyes still burned, and my clothes stuck to my body.

"That man's gonna have to pay for my gear," Daddy mumbled, speeding up.

The chill passed. My back was itching, and I rubbed it against the seat.

We rode in silence most of the way back home. As we turned off Government onto Lafayette Street, I said, "I'm going to start looking for a job right away."

He gave me a questioning look.

"To save up for my motorcycle," I explained. "How much do you think I'll need?"

He didn't answer. And that was okay. There were lots of times he didn't answer. But that also meant he hadn't changed his mind.

"You were drunk!" Mama screamed at him as soon as she understood what had happened.

"It was a storm, Irene," Daddy said. "Came out of nowhere."

She held onto me with both arms, squeezing me against her. She was crying hard.

"What? What?" asked my little brother, Tony. He was nine and as stupid as anybody's little brother.

"Don't ever think about taking either of these boys fishing again," Mama said to him, still holding onto me. "I mean don't ever even think of it."

"I want to go fishing," Tony whined.

"Go change your clothes," Mama said to me.

I peeled off my clothes, toweled myself dry, and quickly dressed. I walked through the kitchen toward the back door. Daddy was taking a bottle of bourbon from the cabinet.

"Give me that," Mama said, grabbing for the bottle.

"Get away, woman," he said, shoving her with his shoulder.

I was out the door fast and ran to the huge pecan tree with the whitewashed trunk that stood in the middle of the backyard. I climbed up to my "thinking limb."

There was a shout and the sound of something crashing from inside the house.

I looked toward the shed beside the garage where Daddy used to park his motorcycle.

Another crash. Probably a lamp.

I pictured my own Harley parked in the shed.

Could I ride it all the way to Alaska? That was another

one of my plans. Daddy said you could still homestead land in Alaska and could make a living by fishing all summer and hunting all winter.

After a while, everything was quiet inside, and I went back into the house. I wanted to call Sam.

Mama was talking on the phone. She took a draw of her cigarette and said, "I'm furious. They could have drowned. I told him he's never taking George out like that again." She paused a moment, listening, then said, "You know what happened, Mother. It's always the same thing."

Daddy stumbled past me and went into the bathroom.

In a minute Mama hung up the phone and gave me another hug. "I would just die if anything happened to you," she said. She let me go and took another draw on the cigarette and blew the smoke away from me. "He can drown himself if he wants to, but I'm not ever letting you go off with him again. Either you or Tony."

"Daddy said I could buy a motorcycle," I said, picking up the telephone receiver.

She shook her head as she walked away. "Sounds like him. He's an idiot."

Three

That night in bed, motorcycles roared up and down in my mind as I lay first on my back, then on my stomach, back and forth. I don't know what time I finally got to sleep. It seemed I had just drifted off when I heard Grandma.

It was Sunday morning, and I stretched my arms and smiled, thinking of Sam the night before when I told him about the Harley. I could still hear him saying, "I just can't believe it."

Mama was saying something now I couldn't make out. Then Grandma spoke. "You shouldn't have told me if you didn't want me to come, Irene," she said.

"I was just so upset," Mama said.

Grandma only came to visit on Sundays because that was the only day her store was closed. It was a combination grocery store and cafe. Bennett's mother, Elizabeth, cooked, and Grandma did almost everything else.

"Where is he?" she said. By the sound of her voice I knew she was in the hall just outside my door.

"He and Tony are still asleep," Mama said.

Grandma laughed and said in a louder voice, "Well, I've got a brand new dollar bill for each of them when they wake up and give their grandma a kiss." She laughed again.

Mama said something and her voice was muffled. They were going into the kitchen.

I got out of bed. I figured I needed about seventy-five dollars for my Harley and a dollar from her would be a good start.

"There he is," Grandma said when I walked into the kitchen. "Give me a love."

She wrapped both arms around me and squeezed me against herself. Grandma was a large woman, "big boned," she said of herself, and she always smelled of talcum powder.

Mama was pouring coffee into cups.

Grandma gave me a knowing look and said, "It was an angel that saved you, George. One of God's angels swooped down and plucked you out of that water like a brand from the burning."

I smiled. "Looked a whole lot like fishermen to me," I said. I wondered if I should mention the dollar.

"No, no," she said, shaking her head. "I know something about angels, and this has all the marks of angel work."

I thought she was going to tell the story about how she had been saved by an angel when she was a baby. There was a fire. The house burned, and her mother and father were killed. She was then raised by two aunts.

"You want some coffee?" Mama asked me.

"No, ma'am," I said, sitting down at the table. "I'm saving up to buy me a motorcycle, Grandma. A Harley-Davidson. That's what Daddy said I should get."

Grandma frowned and looked at her daughter. "What's this?"

Mama set two cups on the table. "More of Monroe's foolishness. This morning he probably won't even re-member saying it."

"I'm not getting a big one," I said. "Just a 165. And every dollar counts."

There was a familiar twinkle in Grandma's eyes. "Oh, it does, does it? Well, go get me my pocketbook. I dropped it on the sofa in the front room."

As she opened her purse and began to fish around for her money, she said, "I've got a plan, Irene. I thought and I thought all the way driving down here this morn-ing." She pulled out the dollar bill and gave it to me.

I thanked her and went into my bedroom to find a place I could hide it so Tony wouldn't find it. I could still hear them talking.

"But you're at the store all day," Mama said. "I just don't see how this is supposed to work."

"Like I told you, I think it would be good for him to get away for a while. And I'm all by myself in that house. It would be good for me, too. And maybe it would give you a chance to think things through."

There was a King Edward cigar box on the shelf at the top of my closet. Too high for Tony to reach. I took a ballpoint pen and wrote on the front of the lid, "I will kill anybody who opens this box," put the dollar inside, and replaced the box. I put a stack of old comics on top of it and went back into the kitchen.

"Tell me what you think about this, George," Grandma said. "I want you to come spend some time in Obadiah with me. Would you like that? You can work for me. A dollar a day, six days a week."

That was six dollars a week. How many weeks in the summer? I needed to look at the calendar, but I was sure I could have close to seventy-five dollars before school started. "Sure," I said.

Mama was frowning. "I'm not sure, Mother," she said.

"I need him, Irene," Grandma said, looking at Mama. "I really do."

Mama smiled and put her hand on her mother's hand. "Maybe for a couple of weeks. Then we'll see how it's going."

Grandma looked at me. "Maybe you could help Bennett some. He's working on the farm for me. There's always something to do."

"I'd rather he just worked at the store," Mama said.

"All right then. He can work at the store. You wouldn't believe how busy it gets some days. Of course, Esther helps Elizabeth at noon, but I still need somebody to bus tables and wash dishes."

Mama glanced up at the doorway to the hall and frowned. I turned my head. Daddy was standing there. His eyes were puffy and his hair uncombed. He'd put on a dry shirt and pair of pants after we got in last night, and he was still wearing them.

"Good morning, Monroe," Grandma said. Her voice was flat. She and Daddy never had much to say to each other. She called him Monroe, but I never heard him use her name when he addressed her. Her name was Tilly Grant, but he never said "Tilly" or "Mrs. Grant" or anything.

He mumbled good morning and went into the bathroom.

Mama took a sip of her coffee, set the cup down, and looked at me. "Okay," she said. "Let's give it a try."

We left for Obadiah in the middle of the afternoon in Grandma's 1947 Ford. The trip took almost three hours. On the way up, she told me again about finding Granddaddy last November 2. "The doctor said he never knew what hit him," she said. "Massive heart attack."

He'd been working too hard, especially these last few years since Staple had run off and he didn't have anyone to help him. She said she'd kept after him to hire someone else, but he had it in his mind that Staple was coming back.

Now, a neighbor, Mr. Vorhise, was looking after her cows. She said he was a bit strange and standoffish, but he seemed to be doing a good job. She had Bennett helping him.

When we arrived at Grandma's, I took my suitcase off of the backseat and closed the door. Immediately, a puppy jumped up on me, hitting his paws on my legs and wagging his tail.

Grandma laughed. "That's Dog," she said.

I followed her toward the house.

"A woman at church gave him to me a couple months ago," she continued. "She thought he might keep me company. Maybe you can think of a name that's better than Dog."

I put my suitcase in Mama's old room and went

back into the front room. On the mantle over the fireplace was a collection of photographs I always like to look at. There was one of Granddaddy. He was young and wearing his World War I uniform and smiling.

His long arms dangled at his sides, and I looked closely at his hands. He had big hands, tanned and bony with huge knuckles and palms so callused that he would just grab a fish without worrying about the fins stabbing him.

There was a picture of Grandma's aunts, Glendora and Olivia, whom she lived with growing up, and pictures of her son, my uncle Matthew, in his merchant marines uniform and of Mama when she graduated from high school, and of me and of Tony. There wasn't a picture of Daddy.

Right in the middle of all the pictures was a small silver-framed photograph of Auntie Nob. Grandma's house was the only house I'd ever been in where there was a picture of a colored person right there in the middle of all the family pictures.

"She was the one who really raised me," Grandma answered one time when I asked about the woman in the picture. Auntie Nob was sitting in a rocker with a blackgum snuff stick protruding from her mouth. She worked for Grandma's two aunts. "She was as close as a mama to me. She was the one who taught me everything really important about living."

I looked back at the picture of Granddaddy and put

my hand gently on the glass. I always loved it when he smiled like that.

I went out into the backyard. The rooster cocked his head and stared at me for a moment, then strutted off behind three hens. The puppy started jumping up on me again, and I bent down and scratched him behind the ears. He kept trying to lick my face.

I walked through the barn and breathed the familiar smells of manure and dry hay and animals and thought of Granddaddy. He loved his cows and talked about them all the time, gave them names, and even smelled a bit like a cow.

I took a deep breath, pulling the smells of the barn inside my head and heart. It was as if I was pulling Granddaddy down deep inside me, and I felt better.

I went out of the barn. The rooster had returned and was watching me. I stood perfectly still. I didn't like roosters, never had since Esther told me and Bennett about one that killed a boy. She said it jumped up on his head and spurred him right behind the ear.

Esther said the rooster had been hexed by Auntie Hoosilla, and that's why it attacked. She said Auntie Hoosilla particularly didn't like little boys.

Auntie Hoosilla was an old hoodoo woman who lived out in the woods somewhere on Grandma's land. I had been terrified of her since I was about four when she stopped in Grandma's backyard and stared at me. She had a dog on a leash with her. The dog was as scrawny as she was and wore a pink bow. Auntie Hoosilla didn't say anything to me. She just stared. After a while, she walked away with the dog trotting beside her.

Esther said whenever Auntie Hoosilla wanted to, she could send mojo power into a creature—dog, cat, cow, hornet, snake, rooster—and control it, make it do whatever she wanted.

I moved cautiously away from the barn, keeping an eye on the rooster. He twisted his head. His black eyes were shining and looking right at me.

He raised one foot, and I froze. My palms were cold and sweating.

Dog came scampering up to my legs, and the rooster turned and moved away.

I eased toward the house. The rooster watched.

I saw a small rock on the ground about the size of a marble. I knelt down slowly, my eyes still on the rooster, and took the rock in my hand.

I stood, threw the rock at the rooster as hard as I could, and jerked around and ran for the back porch. I could tell even before I turned that the rock had missed him entirely.

Four

In the morning I went outside right after I got dressed. Dog danced around in front of me, wanting to play. I reached down and patted him on the rump. I didn't see the rooster.

Bennett was just beyond the outhouse washing a chamber pot. He had certain chores to do around Grandma's before going to help Mr. Vorhise on the farm. He was the same age as me but already was doing man work.

He was wearing faded overalls and no shirt, and I was startled at how much, just for a moment, he looked like his father—broad shouldered with long, sinewy arms. He was much lighter than Staple, however, more of a caramel color. Esther was dark like their father, as dark as a Hershey bar.

He glanced up at me as I approached, then poured another bucket of water over the pot and set it on a fence post to dry. "I didn't expect y'all up till next month," he said.

I followed him toward the chicken house. "I came by myself. I'm going to work for Grandma at the store."

He looked surprised. "Well, well, well," he said, smiling. "Ain't sassy Esther gonna be berserked."

"What?" I asked. I had no idea what he was talking about.

"She be like a crazy person these days, working three jobs," he said, ducking into the chicken house. He swung out the bag of feed and began refilling the feeders. "All she thinks about is money, money, money. All the time. And she asked Miss Tilly about working more at the store than just at lunchtime, and Miss Tilly say there wasn't that much work." He chuckled. "Yessir. She gonna be berserked."

"Grandma must have changed her mind," I said, feeling very uncomfortable at the idea of Esther berserked.

"Wish I had a job like that," he continued. "Anything be better than working for that crazy Mr. Vorhise. Talk about mean? The devil hisself could learn a few lessons from him. Not a day goes by he don't ask me if I wants to come over to his house and play with his dogs."

"What dogs?"

Bennett put the feed sack back into the chicken house and looked at me. "The man raises fighting dogs. He wants them dogs to tear me to pieces. Besides, he killed a man once."

"What?"

He shrugged. "That's all I know."

The back door opened and Grandma stepped out

onto the porch. "George, breakfast is on the table," she said. "'Morning, Bennett."

He nodded and took the chamber pot off the fence post and walked with me to the house.

After breakfast, I went with Grandma to open the store, which was hardly a stone's throw from her house. It was a frame building with a porch across the front and gasoline and kerosene pumps standing slightly to the left side of the porch. In the summer, older men came and sat on the porch in the afternoon. In winter, they sat around the pot-bellied stove inside.

Elizabeth arrived shortly after we got there and began making preparations for lunch. She grinned her big gap-toothed smile when she saw me and said Bennett had just told her I was going to be helping at the store. Elizabeth was bigger even than Grandma and was wearing a green cotton dress with little white flowers on it.

She had come to work for Grandma when she was sixteen, just before she and Staple got married. It was the first time she'd worked inside and not in the field, Grandma said, and at first she was so shy she never said more than yessum and no'm. But that was twenty years ago, and she talked plenty now, especially about her children and her church. According to Grandma, they were her world. Her children and her church. Grandma also said she didn't mention Staple that much anymore.

"You too skinny, George," Elizabeth said to me with a laugh as she walked into the kitchen. "We gonna fleshen you out this summer. Yes, we are."

Grandma went over a list of my daily duties: sweep the front porch, check around for any soda-pop bottles and put them in the wooden cases beside the drink machine, pick up litter outside, sweep the inside aisles, and use the feather duster on the shelf stock. At lunchtime, she said, I'd bus tables, and, when things were slow later in the day, she'd have me restock the shelves. I was also to pump gasoline and kerosene.

The morning passed quickly. Shortly before eleven o'clock, Esther arrived to help Elizabeth through the lunch hour. She walked past me without speaking or even looking at me. I noticed she was as tall as her mother now.

Workmen came in for lunch, Grandma took orders, Elizabeth cooked, and Esther served plates. Most folks wanted the blue plate special—meatloaf, vegetables, and cornbread—with ice tea. I cleared and wiped tables and washed dishes. The kitchen was very hot.

Shortly after one o'clock, Bennett came in and sat down on a ladderback chair at the back of the kitchen. He ate dinner every day at the store, then returned to work on the farm.

Esther put her hands on her hips and smiled a taunting smile at him. "How's your arm?" she asked.

"Leave your brother alone," Elizabeth said. She was wiping down the long table beside the stove.

Bennett ignored Esther. "You want to go fishing this evening?" he asked me.

Esther was still smiling. She sauntered toward the table. "This morning I told a wasp to sting him, Georgie," she said to me. "Just 'cause I felt like it."

"That wasp didn't have nothing to do with you, Midnight Face," he said. Whenever Bennett really wanted to rile her, he called her Midnight Face.

She bristled and stepped toward him.

"Stop all that!" Elizabeth said. "Y'all get your plates and cut out that foolishness."

The three of us took our plates out onto the back porch and sat at a rickety table. Grandma and Elizabeth ate in the kitchen so Grandma could hear if any customers came in.

"Is it still swollen?" Esther asked Bennett, smiling again.

"I swears," Bennett said, taking a bite of cornbread. "Someday they gonna be calling you Auntie Hooesther." He laughed, almost choking on the cornbread, and quickly took a drink of tea. His reference was, of course, to Auntie Hoosilla.

"And if I get like her, I'll have the power to send out a whole swarm of wasps after you every livelong day," Esther said.

She looked at me, tilting her head back slightly so she could look down at me. "So, Georgie," she said, "Just how much Miss Tilly gonna pay you anyways?"

"A dollar a day," I said, hating to have to tell her.

"Humph," she said curling her lip. "I do believe what we got here is a full-blown case of nepotism. Do you know what "nepotism" is, Georgie?" She pronounced each syllable of nepotism slowly, carefully.

I felt my face flushing. She knew I didn't, wouldn't, know a word like that. And I hated her calling me Georgie, and she knew that, too. She'd done it all my life. She got that name from the nursery rhyme, and when we were little, she used to chant, "Georgie Porgie, pudding and pie . . ." over and over again at me.

She looked at Bennett. "What are you smirking about?" she asked. "You don't know what it means either."

"What I know is that you don't make nearly that much in spite of all them jobs you racing around doing. You don't even make fifty cents a day." He snorted. "You might as well forget all your crazy ideas. You ain't never gonna earn enough to—"

"Hush your face," she said. "You don't know how much I make."

"It ain't gonna be enough no ways," he said.

Elizabeth leaned out the back door, holding the screen open. "Esther, it's almost one-thirty. Miz Hannerfield 'spects you right away."

Bennett leaned toward me and said, "The queen here is also a cleaning woman." He laughed.

When we were little, Esther always wanted to play Queen Esther from the Bible. Me and Bennett had to be her slaves. She insisted we call her "Queen Esther" and bow down to her. She'd threaten to whack us if we didn't play.

Esther glared at him for a moment, then said, "Tomorrow morning ... two wasps."

She stood and picked up her plate. "We are glad to have you here, Georgie," she said. "Which bedroom you sleeping in, by the way?"

"What?"

"It wouldn't do for me to send one of my snake friends into Miss Tilly's bed now, would it?" She laughed as she opened the screen door. "Of course, I know you're staying in your mama's room." She laughed again as she went inside.

In the middle of the afternoon, a man stepped into the store. He was a big man, bulky, with his belly rolling over his belt. His straw hat had a dark sweat ring around it, and he was chewing on an unlit cigar. There was an amused expression on his face.

Grandma walked quickly into the kitchen for a moment, then reappeared and said to him, "Can I help you?"

I noticed her voice seemed strained, unnatural.

He stood near the counter by the cash register, slowly looking around. His eyes fell on me and he raised a questioning eyebrow. He turned back to Grandma. "You got any beer?" he asked with a chuckle.

"You know we don't sell beer," she said sharply.

He looked back at me. "And who are you, son?" he asked. "I don't think I know you."

"George Harrington," I said, the words sticking slightly in my throat.

"George Harrington," he repeated. "Well now. You must be Monroe's boy. That right?"

I nodded. "Yes, sir."

"Me and your daddy been buddies for a long time. Yes, we have. Yes, indeed."

He leaned slightly against the counter and craned his neck trying to see into the kitchen.

Grandma moved to block his view.

He scratched the side of his chin and gave her a derisive smile. "Well, I guess since you ain't got no beer, I'll just take five of those big King Edwards."

She took his money, rang up the sale, and gave him the cigars.

Once he was out the door, Grandma darted into the kitchen again.

Five

"Of course, she's upset," said Grandma after we closed the store at six and started walking home. "It's always upsetting to her when that McInnis man comes to the store."

She explained that Leroy McInnis got into a situation with Staple and Elizabeth a long time ago. "It was even before Winston was born. They were just walking down the road coming home from town one Saturday afternoon and a carload of drunk white men came by. The car stopped and the men wanted Elizabeth to go riding with them."

She paused, and I could see she was very uncomfortable talking about it. She continued, "Anyways, Elizabeth and Staple tried to ignore the men and walked on, but the car kept following them. Finally, two of the men got out of the car and started fighting with Staple. They knocked him down and kicked him again and again. Then they got back into the car, laughing and yelling, and drove off. Staple was terribly beaten. One of those two men was Leroy McInnis."

She paused and squinted toward the sun. It was still high and hot. "What I'm telling you the children don't know," she said.

I nodded that I understood that I was not to repeat anything.

She continued. "Your grandfather was furious and went to the sheriff. The sheriff talked to the men and they said Staple got uppity with them, that he'd said something or other, and that they were just trying to be friendly to begin with. The sheriff told Staple to watch his step. Robert exploded all the more. He rarely got like that, but he could get furious. It was all I could do to keep him from going after those men. In fact, Elizabeth begged him to let it rest. She didn't want any more trouble." Grandma shook her head gravely. "That Leroy McInnis is mean. He went to prison for shooting a man, and it looks like he's no different now than when he went in."

I opened the gate to the picket fence in front of the house and we started up the walk.

"With Staple gone now, Elizabeth feels scared lots of times," she said. "Of course, Winston is almost a man, but he's more of a worry than a help to her." She sighed wearily as she climbed the steps. "She doesn't deserve all this. No, indeed."

Grandma made tuna fish sandwiches for supper, and we sat at the kitchen table to eat.

"You ever get any snakes in the house?" I asked.

"Snakes?" she said in a surprised voice.

"Just wondered," I said, picking up my glass of milk.

She smiled and said, "Oh. Esther, huh?"

I made a face but didn't say anything.

"Don't pay her any mind. She's just full of herself these days." She went on to tell me that Esther had just graduated from the colored school in Obadiah as valedictorian. She'd never made below an A in any subject, was homecoming queen, and had starred on the girls' basketball and track teams.

"It's just that the colored school here only goes through the eighth grade," she continued. "Esther has got it in her mind to go to the Negro high school in Adamstown. It's the only one in the county. But Elizabeth doesn't have any kin in Adamstown that Esther can stay with. Their pastor, Reverend Mann, says she can get room and board from a woman he knows there, and Esther is determined to earn enough money to take care of the expense. You have to give her credit."

"Bennett says she's going to be just like Auntie Hoosilla someday."

Grandma gave me a stern look. "No, George," she said solemnly. "Don't say that. Her name is Drusilla Cardamone. You either speak of her as Auntie Drusilla or Miss Cardamone."

I chewed on a bite of my sandwich and didn't say anything.

She reached out her hand and put it on my hand. "I'm glad you came, George. I really am glad." She patted my hand, then wiped her mouth with her napkin and gave a little laugh. "I am sure glad that angel rescued you, too."

"I told you it was some fishermen, Grandma."

"No, no," she said. "It was an angel. Just like it was an angel that rescued me."

"How do you know it was an angel?"

"Auntie Nob told me. It was at night when the fire broke out. Auntie Nob came running up to the house. She just stood there looking at the flames jumping out the windows, and folks were dashing all over the place trying to get buckets and all. Then, she said, she saw it. She saw the whole thing."

"What? What did she see?"

Grandma leaned back in her chair and spoke slowly, carefully. "Then, she said, she saw an angel swoop down from heaven, go right through that front door, and, in a moment, it swooped out again and took me to the grove and left me there. Then it was gone."

"How do you really know that's what she saw?" I asked.

Grandma looked at me as if she couldn't believe what I'd just asked. "How do I know? I know because Auntie Nob told me. And that's the way it was."

There was a knocking at the back door.

"That'll be Bennett," I said. "We're going fishing."

"Just watch out for snakes," she said.

"What?"

She smiled. "At the pond, of course."

Bennett had brought two cane poles and a straightened out wire coat hanger for a stringer. We filled a coffee can with red worms that we'd dug from the soft, cool black dirt on the north side of the barn, just like Granddaddy and Staple had taught us when we were little. It seemed everything we knew about fishing at the pond they'd taught us.

The bright late-afternoon sun swarmed over the face of the still water. A cow drinking on the other side of the dam raised her head and eyed us for a moment, then lowered her head to the water again.

We baited our hooks quickly and began fishing in a cove on the west side. Within the first fifteen minutes Bennett had caught three nice bream, each as big as a man's hand. I'd had my bait stolen a couple of times, but I had yet to land a fish.

Bennett slipped a fish onto the wire stringer, rinsed his hands in the water and dried them on his pants legs, and groaned.

"What's the matter?" I asked. I was getting another bite.

"She can't ever just leave us alone," he said, motioning behind us with his head.

I glanced back and saw Esther strolling down the

hillside, stretching out her long legs like some kind of strutting hen, her hands clasped behind her back. She stopped behind us.

Neither Bennett nor I said anything. He baited his hook again and dropped his line into the water.

"Georgie Porgie, I was wondering how long you planning on staying," she said.

"Don't pay any attention to her," Bennett said. "She just thinks if you don't stay, Miss Tilly will give her your job."

"Hush up," she said to him. "You don't know what I think. Sand can't think, and that's all your ugly head is filled with anyway. Mushy sand." She stepped closer to me. "I asked you a question, Georgie Porgie."

She walked closer and stood right next to me. Her face was only inches from the side of my face. "By the way," she said in almost a whisper. "You seen Miss Tilly's rooster?"

"Yes," I said, wishing I could think of something smart to say.

"How did he look?"

"Look?"

"Probably it ain't important." She was so close I could hear her breathing. "Only I seen Auntie Hoosilla passing through Miss Tilly's backyard the other day and she stopped and looked at that rooster a long time. He didn't bat an eye or move, I'm telling you, till she walked on."

"She's lying," said Bennett, drawing up his pole and swinging another flopping fish to the grassy bank.

Esther turned abruptly to her brother. Her fists were clenched. "You calling me a liar?" she asked.

Bennett raised one shoulder as if ready to ward off a blow. "I ain't said you was a liar," he said. "I only said you was lying. That's not the same thing."

She looked back at me and smiled. "Mind you, I ain't said she had hexified him, but I'd be careful when I had to go through the backyard. In fact, I don't think I'd plan on staying in Obadiah too long, Georgie."

"Even if you was working at the store you still wouldn't make enough money to go to whatever fool place you thinks you is going," Bennett said to Esther. He looked at me. "She thinks she gonna ride a bus up to New York City or Detroit during fall break."

All of the colored schools let out the first of October for six weeks so the children can help with the cotton harvest. Even the white schools used to let out, Grandma said, when Mama and Daddy were growing up.

The idea of traveling anywhere—especially some place as exotic as New York City or Detroit—was exciting to me. "Are you serious?" I asked Esther.

She didn't reply. Her attention was fixed on her brother. "You don't know what I'm going to do," she said.

Bennett made a contemptuous snort. "She thinks she's gonna find Daddy and—"

"Shut up!" she said, interrupting him. Her lower lip

trembled. "I don't understand what happened, but I know he can explain everything."

Bennett's eyes had a glazed look as he stared across the pond. "Sure," he said.

Esther turned and hurried back up the hill. I thought I'd seen tears in her eyes.

Six

The next morning after breakfast, Dog followed Grandma and me as we walked to the store. Grandma said it would be all right if he came along, but we might have to tie him up if he got underfoot.

Every time I went outside to put gas in a car or fill someone's kerosene can, I petted Dog. He found himself a place under the bench on the porch and napped. Whenever a customer arrived, he jumped up and wagged his tail, expecting to be petted.

After the second time he got into the store, Grandma had me tether him to one of the porch posts.

About halfway through the lunch hour, I looked up from the sink and saw Winston coming into the kitchen. He was sixteen now, as tall as a man and thick chested. He had a deep scar on the side of his face from a fight he'd been in the year before. Bennett told me somebody had cut him with a broken beer bottle.

Winston was with another boy, Jonathan Spears. He looked about the same age as Winston. They both wore faded and patched denim overalls that were sprinkled with sawdust from the mill where they worked.

Esther always said you had to be as careful around Winston as you would be around a rattlesnake, and I agreed.

Once when I was very small he locked me up in the toolshed. I was terrified. After a while he let me out and told me he'd kill me if I told Grandma. I never had.

Winston now hung out with some rough men around a colored pool hall in town called the Blue Note. He wouldn't be doing that, Grandma said, if Staple was still around, and Elizabeth worried herself sick all the time about him.

Elizabeth smiled when she noticed Winston. She placed a plate on the ledge for Grandma to take to a customer and said to him, "Y'all had dinner?"

"Yessum," Winston said, grinning and walking over to her. He put his arms around her and squeezed.

"Lemme go," she said. "I gots work to do." But I could see the glow in her eyes. Grandma once told me Elizabeth loved that boy more than life itself.

"I just wanted to know if you wants to go for a ride in my car," he said.

She looked at him sideways. "Car? What car?"

He laughed. "That big brand new Pontiac I gonna buy me someday."

Elizabeth shook her head and gave him a big smile as she served up another plate. "You sure you ain't hungry?"

Jonathan walked closer to Esther and gave her a jaunty smile. She moved away from him.

"I need you to loan me a dollar till I get paid Friday," Winston said to his mother.

She gave him the money, and he and Jonathan left just as Bennett came in.

"I see your lover boy was just here," he said to Esther when Winston and his friend were gone.

"Shut your fool mouth," she said.

"Hush up. Both of you," said Elizabeth. "And I don't want to tell you again not to call your brother a fool, girl." Elizabeth put one hand on her hip. "You hear me?"

"Yes, ma'am," Esther answered with emphasis on the "ma'am." It was a word I rarely heard her say.

In the middle of the afternoon when I was stamping prices on new Campbell's soup cans, a man I'd never seen before came into the store. He was wearing a denim shirt and khaki pants and a slouch hat, and he didn't look much taller than me. His nose was crooked like a boxer's and his cheeks sunk deep into his face. He stopped just inside the door and looked at me with cold gray eyes.

I nodded in greeting. He didn't nod back.

Grandma came from around the counter. "Mr. Vorhise, do you know my grandson, George?" she asked.

I walked over and shook his hand.

He turned to Grandma. "I'm going over to the back side of your land to check the fence. I'll have the boy run the fence line and nail the wire back wherever it's come loose," he said. "Have you decided how many head you want me to take to market?"

"No," Grandma said. "I'll let you know in a day or two."

"And I need some gas. Two dollars worth."

Grandma nodded at me and I went outside.

Mr. Vorhise's pickup truck was parked beside the gas pump. Bennett was sitting in the back of the truck on one side. He didn't look at me or say anything.

As I unscrewed the gas cap, a dog thudded against the side window of the truck, snarling and barking at me. Bennett jumped to his feet and spun around toward the cab.

I took a step back.

"It's one of his crazy fighting dogs," he said. "Every time Mr. Vorhise opens the door, my heart is ready to stop."

I began filling the tank. The dog continued barking. Its hair bristled and its eyes were fearsome.

"What kind of dog is it?" I asked.

"Just some dog from hell. Ain't no regular kind. Breeded just to kill. And it just as soon kill a human being as another dog."

Mr. Vorhise came out onto the porch just as the pump showed two dollars. I replaced the nozzle and screwed the cap back on.

He lit a cigarette and stepped off the porch. "You like my dog?" he asked.

I walked around the back of the truck. "Yes, sir," I said.

Dog, still tethered to the porch post, was looking toward the truck and the din coming from the cab. His ears were raised and he was completely still. Except when he was sleeping, I'd never seen him still.

I stepped beside him and put one hand on his chest as I scratched his head. His heart was racing.

Mr. Vorhise opened the driver's-side door, and his dog sprang out and lunged toward me and Dog.

I flinched.

As the fighting dog reared up, I saw Mr. Vorhise had him by a chain. The dog was straining, jerking against the chain. Saliva sprayed from his mouth.

Dog curled behind my legs and whimpered. I picked him up in my arms.

Mr. Vorhise began laughing. "Can that dog of yours fight?" he asked me.

"Sir?"

The man's feet were planted in the dust, and he was leaning back against the chain as the dog jerked at it. "Just put it down on the ground for a minute," he said. "Let's just see what it does. I won't let it get hurt."

I glanced up at the bed of the truck. Bennett's eyes were enormous. He was still standing.

"No, sir," I said softly.

I reached down and untied the rope from the post. My fingers were shaking. I stood up again, and, holding Dog against my chest, I went back into the store.

I could hear Mr. Vorhise laughing as he forced his dog back into the cab.

Grandma was on the phone, taking down an order.

I began to tremble all over.

She hung up the phone and looked at me. "What on earth . . . ?"

My breathing was jerky. "Mr. Vorhise wanted me to let Dog fight his dog," I said.

She walked to the doorway. The pickup was already gone. She shook her head slowly and walked back. "He's gone now," she said.

"I hear he killed a man once," I said.

Grandma picked up a basket and the order pad. "No, that's not right. The man didn't die." She placed a pound can of Luzianne Coffee and Chicory into the basket. "It was over in Mississippi in one of those road-houses. Apparently he got in a fight with another man. The man got hurt bad. Real, real bad. Now he's para-lyzed from the neck down. Both of them were drunk, as I understand it. Mr. Vorhise says he doesn't drink anymore, and I told him I was willing to give him a chance working my stock, but the first time I ever see him drunk we are through."

She put a can of corned beef and two cans of pine-apple into the basket, then paused and glanced toward the kitchen. "I think Elizabeth worries some about Bennett working for him. She's afraid one of those dogs might get loose." She carried the basket to the counter. "When I finish filling this basket, you can take it to Mrs. Cooper."

I took Dog back out onto the porch and tied him up again. I walked out beside the gas pump and looked down the road toward the turn-off I knew Mr. Vorhise would have taken to drive Bennett to the back side of Grandma's property. A fury began rising up inside me.

I wished I was already a man, grown and strong. I would have shown that Mr. Vorhise what a fight was all about.

Seven

Wednesday and Thursday Esther didn't eat with me and Bennett on the porch. She ate inside with Elizabeth and Grandma.

On Friday, however, she brought out her plate and sat down at the table with us. She had not spoken a word to either one of us in two days.

She looked at her brother. "Weren't you telling me last winter about some cave you came across rabbit hunting? Where was that?"

He looked confused for a moment, then answered, "It was over at the northeast corner of Miss Tilly's property."

"That would be the corner right up against Vorhise land, wouldn't it?"

"So?"

She jerked her head toward the kitchen. "Miss Tilly and Mama was just now talking and Miss Tilly said Mr. Vorhise is related to the Chisms. The bank-robbing Chisms. Did you know that? His mother was the daughter of one of them, so that means Mr. Vorhise's grandfather was one of the bank-robbing Chisms!"

"So?" he said again.

She looked at me. "Did you know that?"

I shook my head. I hadn't known that, but I did know about the bank-robbing Chism brothers. Granddaddy used to tell me stories about their escapades when Grandma wasn't listening.

There were three of them, and they went on a rampage, robbing banks and killing lawmen during the late 1890s before they were caught near Obadiah and hanged in a huge oak tree on the other side of town. Granddaddy said his father saw the hangings.

When the brothers were captured, however, they didn't have any of the money they'd stolen, and they refused to tell where they'd hidden it. It was thought that they'd squirreled it away in the woods someplace.

Esther glanced up at the back door of the store, then leaned forward. There was a gleam in her eyes, and she spoke in a lower voice. "Now listen. All of us got to work this afternoon, but tomorrow is Saturday, and we get off early, and . . ." Her voice trailed off and she smiled knowingly at each of us.

Bennett frowned. "What you talking about?" he asked.

"I'm talking about bank-robbers' money, fool face," she whispered sternly. "Where better to hide it than a cave?" She paused, slowly nodding her head. She was no longer smiling.

Bennett and I exchanged glances.

"Okay?" she demanded, looking at each of us in turn.

I nodded.

Bennett looked skeptical. "We split it three ways?" he asked.

"Of course," she said, standing up. She turned to go, then paused and looked back at us. She pointed her finger at Bennett and said, "Don't say a word about this to anyone." Then she pointed at me. "Don't even tell your grandmother."

"I wouldn't anyway," I said.

"Miss Tilly closes the store at four on Saturday. We can leave then and still have more than three hours of daylight."

We both nodded.

After she left, Bennett said, "If we find that money, George, you can buy as many motorcycles as you want."

"What will you do with your money?"

He leaned over the side of the porch and spit into the dirt. "The first thing is I'm gonna quit cleaning slop jars for your grandmother. And the second thing is I'm buying me a horse. I don't know beyond that."

The door pushed open, and Elizabeth leaned out. "Bennett, Mr. Vorhise is out front in his pickup blowing the horn. You hurry on now 'fore you upset him."

Bennett made a face, gathered up his plate and glass, and went back into the kitchen.

I finished my milk, then followed him inside. I could hardly wait for tomorrow.

Eight

The next day, shortly before four o'clock, Grandma told me I could go, that she would close up the store by herself. I ran home. Bennett and Esther were waiting for me in the backyard. Bennett had a short-handled shovel on his shoulder. Esther was carrying two white candles.

We set out at once with Dog close behind.

Bennett led us down the rut-scarred single-lane road that ran flush beside Grandma's house and downhill to a row of cabins, the first of which was the home of Elizabeth and her three children. The next one was vacant and had been for years, and the third was rented by the Armstrong family, who farmed on shares for Grandma.

"What if we do find that money?" Bennett said. "Won't we just have to give it back to the bank?"

"The bank's got insurance for things like that," Esther said. "They already got their money back. Besides, if we did have to give it back, they'd probably give us a reward big enough to do whatever we need to do."

I agreed. Maybe I would have enough to buy a new 165. All I'd considered to this point was a used one. A very used one.

The road stopped beyond the Armstrong house and became a cow trail. Bennett led us up the trail, then through a stretch of tall grass and into the woods. There was no discernible path.

We walked up and down hills thick with tall oaks, sweetgums, elms, sycamores, and an occasional magnolia. We jumped across two small streams and walked on a fallen log over a larger stream.

At one point, Dog stopped and turned around, looking behind us, listening. His ears were up, and he was perfectly still.

"Here, Dog," I called back to him. Esther and Bennett were striding on ahead.

"Just come on," Bennett called back to me. "He'll come."

I walked on, looking back to see if he would follow. He darted after me, but stopped every few feet to stare back into the forest as if he heard something following us.

"Are we still on Miss Tilly's land or is this Vorhise land?" Esther asked.

"Hard to say," Bennett said.

"What about his dogs?" I asked. "I mean, how many are there?"

"Four," he answered. "And the devil hisself is in every one of them."

"But they don't just run loose, do they?"

"Not usually," he said. "'Course, sometimes he lets them out to exercise, and they go tearing off all over the place."

"This is Saturday afternoon, and you ain't never around there on Saturday afternoon," Esther said.

We ducked beneath a cluster of low-hanging vines and emerged into a narrow clearing in front of a steep drop.

"The cave's right down there," Bennett said, pointing to the edge of a cliff.

We lowered ourselves over the rocks and dropped down to the lip of the cave. Dog whimpered and made a general fuss trying to get down. He finally crawled near the ledge and lay down. He rested his muzzle on his front legs and watched us.

The cave was low, and we had to squat to go inside. It wasn't more than ten feet deep, and the sun was still high enough for there to be dim light inside. Esther lit the candles anyway.

Bennett took the shovel and started digging in the sandy floor. He turned over shovelfuls of earth quickly. Esther and I knelt beside him, watching. After a few minutes, he paused and said, "They could have hidden that money anywheres. Why would they hide it here?"

"Give me that shovel," Esther said, pulling it from him. "All you do is complain."

Suddenly there was a loud, sharp yelp from Dog. I scrambled outside and looked up the hill.

Dog saw me emerge from the cave and leaped up. He bounced along the rocks, trying to stand on his hind feet. I swept him up in my arms. Esther stepped out and stood beside me.

"What is it, Dog?" I asked.

A figure suddenly loomed up over us at the top of the hill.

I was too stunned to do anything but reach out with one hand to the side of the cliff for balance. My legs were rubbery.

"It's Auntie Hoosilla," Esther whispered just as Bennett stepped out.

The old woman stood facing us. She was wearing a black hood of some sort, and all I could see of her face was a twisted chin. Her tattered dress looked like it was made out of an old croker sack.

"What is it, Auntie Drusilla?" asked Esther.

The old woman moved slowly and carefully down the rocks, coming closer and closer to us. She held her head slightly cocked, reminding me of Grandma's rooster. She didn't move.

"What, Auntie?" asked Esther again.

She didn't answer, didn't make a sound.

I could feel my heart beating faster and faster.

She drew close to us, shuffled past Esther and then Bennett, and stopped directly in front of me.

I couldn't breathe.

She reached up one gnarled hand, its fingers spread

out toward my face, moving it ever closer as if she were going to touch me. I thought I could almost make out a smile.

Suddenly she whirled around, making her loose garments flap, and scooted back up the hillside and disappeared into the trees. I was shaking.

"Why did she do that?" Bennett asked. "Was she hexifying you?"

I couldn't speak.

He turned to his sister. "Did you see her face?" he asked. "I mean, I couldn't see much, but . . ."

"A long time ago she was touched by the devil," said Esther, looking curiously at me. "That's what I heard. The devil ran his hands all over her face as he climbed down into her mind."

"Let's get out of here," Bennett said.

"No," said Esther. "We haven't dug up half the floor in there."

"Then dig it yourself. I'm going." He was already almost up to the top of the hill.

I followed after him, carrying Dog until I stepped onto level ground. I put him down, and he ran on ahead of me.

"It's all mine, then," she called after us. "And I mean it."

We ignored her and continued on through the woods. It was dusk now. I heard an owl.

Bennett paused and listened. He turned his head

slowly, looking carefully at the thick woods in front of us. "She may be anywheres," he said. "She may have even turned herself into something else."

"What else?" I asked. Dog was right at my feet.

He shrugged. "Bat, crow. Maybe even that hoot owl. And, she can kill you with a look. Most likely, though, she'll get some creature to do it. No telling how many peoples she done killed."

He crossed the log over the stream. I gathered up Dog in my arms and followed. Occasionally, as we continued on toward home, I glanced back. I shuddered every time I heard that owl.

When I came to the supper table that evening there were six one-dollar bills fanned out in front of my place and a fifty-cent piece and a dime.

Grandma smiled. "For six days of work," she said. "The sixty cents is a bonus."

I took the bills, folded them, and slipped them into my pocket. Then I picked up the two coins.

"Actually," Grandma said slowly with a smile. "That's your tithe. Ten percent." She held out her hand to me, palm up. "I'll put them in an envelope for you, and you can drop it in the offering plate in the morning."

I gave her the two coins and sat down at the table. She passed me a plate of cheese, leftover field peas, boiled potatoes, and biscuits.

I wasn't hungry at all.

"We were playing out in the woods this evening,"
I said. "And . . . Auntie Drusilla came up."

She smiled. "And what did she say?"

"Nothing."

"She never does."

"Esther said she'd heard Auntie Drusilla is so ugly because the devil put his hands on her face."

"Now, don't you children go bothering that poor old woman. She was probably a lot more afraid of you all than you were of her. And, besides. Who is ever to say who is ugly and who is not? God loves her exactly the way she is. To God she's very beautiful and that's really all that counts."

"Can she . . . can she hexify people?"

Grandma smiled. "I'd rather say she can bless people."

"How do you know that?"

"That's what Auntie Nob told me."

I knew by the way she said it, there was nothing else to say on the matter. I took a bite of my biscuit and tried to chew.

After supper I went into my bedroom and added the six dollars to the one dollar in the cigar box.

After Grandma cleared the table, she gave me a small package of table scraps wrapped in butcher paper. "I thought the puppy might like these," she said, handing me the package.

I walked outside. It was already dark.

"Dog!" I called. "Here, Dog!"

There was silence. Only silence. No movement in the yard. The rooster was not around. The chickens were in their coop.

I walked farther out from the house. "Dog!" I said.

I heard a faint whimper near the barn. I moved carefully toward it.

Dog was near the barbed-wire fence beside the barn.

"What is it, boy?" I asked kneeling down beside him. His tail was between his legs and he kept looking from me toward the field beyond the fence.

I looked toward the field. Something moved. I saw it for only a split second, and then it was gone, just a quick shadow. Auntie Hoosilla? Maybe. I wasn't sure.

Why did she do that back at the cave? What did she want of me?

Nine

The following Saturday, June 25, was my thirteenth birthday. There was a small package at my place at breakfast.

Grandma turned around from the stove and grinned. "Open it," she said. "I think you're going to be surprised."

I pulled off the ribbon and tore loose the paper.

Inside was a pocketknife. I held it in my hand, looking down at it. A Barlow knife. Not a new one but well used. The brown bone handle was worn at the edges.

I looked up at Grandma. "Granddaddy's knife," I said.

She nodded and turned back to the stove. "And I've got another surprise for you later."

I pulled out the knife's main blade. It was honed sharp enough to shave the hairs on my arm. I had seen Granddaddy do that every time he sharpened it— shave a small portion of hair just above his left wrist to see if the knife was sharp enough.

The other surprise was that Grandma let me off

work right after lunch, and she gave Esther, Bennett and me fifty cents each to go to the picture show in town, plus a dime each for popcorn.

Town was only a quarter mile from the store. We were there in plenty of time for the 1:30 matinee.

Esther and Bennett went around to the colored entrance on the side, and I went in at the front. During the "Tom and Jerry" cartoon I thought I could hear Bennett laughing up in the balcony above me. He had a real high-pitched laugh.

The movie was called *Blackboard Jungle*. It was about a big-city high school and a lot of wild teenagers. As I watched it, I kept wishing I was sixteen already and could leave home and go off on my own someplace, that I could hitchhike to a big city like New York or Los Angeles, or join the merchant marines and sail to Japan and Africa and Hawaii.

Afterward, when we came outside into the daylight, it was cloudy, and I heard a rumble of thunder. The air was thick and smelled like rain.

As we were walking back toward home, I told Bennett I could hear him laughing.

"I just love that Jerry," he said with a grin. "And me and Esther got the best seats, right on the front row."

Esther raised up her head a bit and added, "The best seats in the whole place, in fact. You know, you can hear much better in the balcony."

I knew she didn't have any way to compare the balcony with the main-floor seats, any more than I did, and I was going to say so when I heard a vehicle coming up the road behind us. The three of us moved quickly to the side of the road.

It was a pickup, and it slowed down almost to a stop as it drew abreast of us. Inside were two men. The driver was Leroy McInnis. I didn't recognize the other man. He wore a grease-stained cap and was as big as Mr. McInnis.

Mr. McInnis had an unlit cigar clamped between his teeth, just like he'd had at the store. He leered at us, and I wondered if the other man was the one that helped Mr. McInnis beat up Staple. I also wondered if Mr. McInnis knew Esther and Bennett were Elizabeth's children.

I glanced at Bennett and Esther. They were looking straight ahead, their faces like stone.

I looked back at Mr. McInnis. He half grinned, half sneered at me. "I wish your father could see you now, boy," he said. "Wouldn't he be proud."

He raced the motor and the truck lurched forward, kicking up a cloud of dust.

"Who was that?" asked Bennett as we turned our backs and closed our eyes while the cloud rolled over us.

I didn't answer. Grandma said they didn't know about the fight between their father and McInnis, and I sure didn't want to be the one to tell them.

Lightning flashed. It was followed almost immediately by a crash of thunder. Then heavy raindrops began falling. We broke into a run.

By the time we turned onto Catawba Road, rain was

blowing hard, and lightning jumped all around us. Bennett ran toward an abandoned barn on the left side of the road. Esther and I followed.

The roof was gone in the rear of the barn and the rain poured in, but we stood at the doorway in a dry place, looking out. Wind snatched at the limbs of a huge oak tree in the yard, whipping them up and down. A heavy, dead, and leafless limb thudded to the ground not ten feet from the doorway.

"Maybe it's a tornado," yelled Bennett, looking up toward the ceiling of the barn. Water was rushing in nearby. The tin roof groaned as the wind pulled at it.

Esther was smiling. "I love the rain," she said. "And the thunder. God speaks in the thunder, you know."

"Well, he's sure doing a lot of talking now," said Bennett.

"That's right," she said. She closed her eyes, her smile broadening. "Yes, Lord," she whispered. "Speak, Lord."

Bennett looked at me and rolled his eyes.

Suddenly Esther ran outside into the middle of the slashing rain and wind, holding her arms straight up in the air, smiling, and spinning around and around, her bare feet churning in the mud.

"Yes, Lord!" she yelled. "I hear you, Lord!"

She spun faster and faster. The smile vanished and a look of distress moved across her face.

"Please . . . ," she cried, spinning with her arms out straight.

"No!" she screamed. "No, no, no!"

She collapsed into the mud and sat in the rain, gasping for air.

The rain slackened. Bennett and I eased out of the barn, walked past her, and made our way to the road. I glanced back once. Esther was still sitting on the ground.

I think Bennett was as stunned as I was and, like me, wanted to know what terrible thing the Lord had said to her. Neither of us, however, mentioned the matter as we walked home.

Ten

Esther was her regular old mean, sassy self the next day. She didn't act like someone who God would have much to say to.

On Tuesday, Bennett told me he'd asked her what God said last Saturday in the rain, and she first told him to mind his own business. If God wanted him to know, he'd tell him. Bennett told her he didn't think she heard God say anything.

"She didn't say nothing for a long time," he said. "Then finally she said God told her he gonna tell her exactly where Daddy is. That way she'll know whether to go to New York City or Detroit or wherever."

"When is he going to tell her?" I had never known God to talk to anyone who wasn't a preacher.

"She say at the Esther service."

"What's the Esther service?"

He sighed and made a face. "You wouldn't be interested." And that was all he would say.

On Thursday, I was stacking dirty dishes at a table when a large colored man entered the store. He was very dark and wore a wide-brimmed straw hat. He smiled and nodded in my direction, then paused before a table where two men in bib overalls were eating. They were the only two customers left.

"Afternoon, sirs," he said.

Neither returned his greeting or looked up.

"Afternoon, Reverend Mann," said Grandma.

"Afternoon, Miss Tilly," he said, taking off his hat. "God bless you."

"And God bless you, Reverend."

Grandma introduced me to Reverend Russell Mann and explained that he was the pastor of Mount Nebo Baptist Church, the church where Elizabeth, Bennett, Esther, and Winston went.

"I was wondering if Sister Elizabeth is here," he said. The smile had never left his face.

Grandma led him into the kitchen where Elizabeth and Esther were putting food away and washing pots.

I followed with the tray of dirty dishes.

Both Elizabeth and Esther dried their hands and came over to shake hands with their pastor. Esther almost bounded up to him and took his large hand in both of hers. I had never seen her smile bigger.

"I just came to remind y'all about Sunday," he said.

"We know," said Elizabeth. "You always preaches that sermon on the Sunday before July Fourth."

He looked at Grandma. "It's my special Esther sermon," he said. "I invite all the womens named Esther to come to the front pew. We would be greatly honored if you and your grandson would join us Sunday morning. It's going to be a wonderful day."

Grandma glanced at me and said with a smile, "Thank you, Reverend. We just might be there, the Lord willing."

"Who knows?" he said with his eyes on Esther. "Maybe God might speak to somebody in a powerful way."

Esther looked away quickly. There was an uneasy expression in her eyes.

As the preacher was leaving, Bennett came into the kitchen.

"It's time for the Esther sermon," Elizabeth said to him, beaming.

Bennett made a face and said, "Maybe I'll be sick Sunday morning and not have to go to church." He turned and went onto the back porch to wait for us to eat.

Before we went to bed Saturday night, Grandma told me we were going to church at Mount Nebo Baptist.

"I remember how much Staple enjoyed the Esther service," she said. "Sometimes he would sing a solo. My, my, my, but that man could sing."

"Do you think God speaks to people?" I asked. "I mean, just like in the Bible."

"To some people maybe. Some very special people."

In the morning, shortly before eleven o'clock,

Elizabeth, Bennett, and Esther arrived at the back door.

Elizabeth was wearing a white dress and white shoes, and she carried a pair of white gloves in her hand.

Like me, Bennett wore a white short-sleeved shirt and a tie.

Esther looked like I had never seen her before. Her hair was pulled up and her skin was glowing. Her dress was lemon yellow and she wore a straw hat with a yellow ribbon. Her smile was almost nervous.

We rode in Grandma's car to the church. Scattered around in front of the paintless clapboard building were a few battered automobiles and pickups and three wagons with mules.

One mule turned his head and watched us as we entered the building.

Two women ushers, dressed in white, stood just inside the door. One handed Grandma and me each a fan. The other beckoned with her hand for us to follow her. She led Grandma, me, and Bennett down to the second pew from the front on the right side.

Elizabeth sat with the deaconesses in a special section on the other side. Esther sat on the front pew right in front of us. There was no one else in the pew.

The music began and the congregation clapped and swayed and sang for the next hour. Esther rocked gently back and forth, back and forth.

It was stifling hot in the church. All the fresh air

had already been breathed up, and I fanned my face. Printed on the fan were the words "Clayton's Funeral Parlor" and a picture of Jesus.

Finally, Reverend Mann took his place behind the pulpit. He began speaking very slowly, haltingly, in a low voice. He told the story in the Bible about how the Hebrew people were far, far from home in a strange land where they'd been taken as slaves and how the rulers of that land oppressed them. And about how when a contest was held to pick a new queen, a young woman of the Hebrews named Esther was the most beautiful of all and won the contest.

"Then . . . there came an evil man," he said, his voice rising. "An evil man named Haman."

"An evil man," someone said loudly.

The preacher mopped his face with his handkerchief and walked a few steps from the pulpit.

"Take your time," a deacon sitting to the side of the pulpit said. "Take your time."

"This was an evil man, a man determined to destroy God's people," he said, wiping his chin and looking straight at Esther. "But God had himself a deliverer!"

"Yes, he did!" shouted a woman on the other side of Bennett, rising to her feet.

"And Esther's uncle come to her." He was almost shouting now. "He come and he says to her, 'Who knoweth . . .'" He paused and wiped his face again.

"Who knoweth!" someone shouted.

"'Who knoweth,' he says to her . . . ," continued the preacher.

"Yes, he did!"

Sweat was popping out all over Reverend Mann's face, and he spread out his arms and fully extended every finger. His eyes grew to twice their normal size, and he stood right over Esther and roared, "'Who knoweth whether thou art come to the kingdom for such a time as this!'"

"Yes, yes, yes!" shouted someone behind me.

"For such a time as this!" one of the deacons shouted. He was standing, too.

I glanced around. Half the congregation was standing, including Elizabeth, who was stomping her feet. Others held their arms up in the air. Esther was still swaying back and forth.

And quickly then the preacher began telling how Esther brought down the evil Haman who was trying to destroy her people, how she was anointed by God for that special work, and how she was faithful, she was faithful.

He began chanting and singing and moving fast behind the pulpit.

Suddenly Esther stopped swaying. She became very still.

A large woman in a rose-colored dress standing behind me shouted and began to whoop. She moved into the aisle. I tried not to stare, but I couldn't keep my eyes off her. She was dancing with jumps and jerks and shouting.

Two women ushers hurried beside her. One took off the large woman's eyeglasses. They held out their hands toward her, but didn't touch her. Her face glistened with sweat, and her eyes were closed. She continued to shout and jump and whirl around.

She moved across in front of Esther and cried out, "Yes, Lord! Yes, Lord!"

The preacher spun around on the stage and shouted, "Hallelujah!"

I looked at the side of Esther's face. There was a serenity in her eyes as she stared straight ahead. She seemed completely oblivious to the cyclone of holy activity and noises swirling around her. Her body was motionless, and she was deep within herself. I wondered if God was talking to her, and, if he was, what he was saying.

Eleven

The store was closed Monday for the Fourth of July. Grandma said we were going to visit Aunt Glendora and Aunt Olivia and have lunch with them.

Before we left that morning, I went into the backyard to teach Dog how to fetch a stick. I couldn't get Esther and the way she looked in church out of my mind.

She'd said not a word as we drove home from church. Her eyes were rimmed with tears.

Grandma told me at supper that folks responded to God in different ways. Some shouted, and some got quiet. She said she thought those tears in Esther's eyes were probably tears of joy.

I didn't think so.

Grandma came to the door. "I think you'd best tie Dog up so he doesn't follow us," she said. "My aunts have an old dog who probably wouldn't care much for him."

I got a piece of clothesline out of the shed and tethered him to the post beside the back steps. That allowed him to sleep in his special shady spot.

As we neared the house where my great aunts lived, Grandma pointed out the spot next to it where Auntie Nob's cabin had been. It burned down last summer. Auntie Nob, she said, had been dead for fifteen years come this October. "I spent as much time in her cabin as in my own house," she said, smiling.

After we ate lunch, Grandma and her two aunts sat on the porch and told stories of long-dead relatives and friends for what seemed like forever. I tried to interest their dog, Caleb, in playing catch but he just crawled up under the house.

Finally, we headed home.

When we got there, Dog was gone. I stood looking at the rope. One end was still attached to the post. The other was lying on the steps.

"You have to tie up a frisky puppy real good," Grandma said. "I'm sure he's not far."

I walked out by the barn and called and waited. He didn't come. I walked down to the pond and called. No Dog. I went to the fence on the east side separating Grandma's land from Mr. Vorhise's. I sure hoped he hadn't wandered over there. I didn't want to think about what could happen to him if he ran into one of those fighting dogs.

I walked down to the store, thinking maybe Dog got confused and trotted down there looking for us.

When I got back home, Grandma was sitting on the back steps. She was twirling a tiny white flower between her thumb and forefinger.

"Mama calls those angel flowers," I said.

She smiled at me. "She got that name from me, and I got it from Auntie Nob. I picked some in the field one day and brought them home, and Auntie Nob asked me if an angel had given them to me. She said they were angel flowers."

I saw another one on the second-to-bottom step and picked it up. Several more lay on the ground, the delicate white petals resting lightly on the dull brown earth. The wind, no doubt, had blown them in from the field.

Grandma was staring toward the sky.

"Dog wasn't at the store," I said.

She had a faraway look in her eyes. "He'll be all right."

"But what if somebody picks him up and doesn't know where he belongs?"

She shrugged. "Then they can give him a nice home," she said. "God will take care of Dog, just like God takes care of us."

I looked toward the barn and the cow trail that led to the pond. Maybe he was running rabbits. Maybe Bennett was at the pond, and Dog had followed him.

I left Grandma without saying a word. It bothered me that she didn't seem to care about Dog being gone. She didn't care one bit.

Twelve

Dog wasn't at the pond. I walked around in the fields and to the edge of the woods calling his name, but I never heard him. Not a yelp, not a bark. Nothing.

I got up early the next morning hoping he'd come home during the night. He hadn't. I asked Grandma if we could ride around in the car and look for him. She said maybe later, that dogs could take care of themselves, and for me to stop fretting.

"I want to talk with you and Bennett and Esther at lunchtime," she said. "I've got a big job for y'all."

While we were eating she came out onto the porch. "The church's homecoming is the third Sunday in August," she said, "and I want some fish to fry. Lots of fish. I want my locker at the icehouse full of fish." Homecoming was when the church cemetery was cleaned up and folks who had moved away came back and there was a big dinner-on-the-grounds.

Grandma said she was willing to pay a nickel a piece for good-sized fish. "No runty fish," she said. "Good fish."

Esther's eyes got bright at once, and when Grandma went back inside, she leaned forward and whispered with a grin, "Come October, I'm going to New York."

"It's New York then?" asked Bennett.

She shook her head and wouldn't say anything else.

Business that afternoon was as sluggish as the heat. About four o'clock, I was stamping prices on bleach when I heard the screen door open. Coming in the door was none other than Auntie Hoosilla. I felt my heart jump into racing gear.

She paused just inside the door. She seemed much smaller than I remembered from that day at the cave. In fact, she was hardly five foot tall and looked almost frail in her baggy clothes. Of course, I knew her strength wasn't in her muscles, but in her evil eye. Because a hood shrouded her face completely, I couldn't see her eyes, or even her face.

I knew I had to avoid looking at her with more than a glance at a time or else she might lock onto my eyes with her eyes and hexify me, but I desperately wanted to watch her.

She walked in jerks toward the counter where Grandma sat working on monthly statements.

Grandma stood up at once and smiled at her. "Good afternoon, Auntie," she said. "Let me help you."

Auntie Hoosilla said not a word.

Grandma picked up a basket and moved around the

counter. "You need fruit," she said. "Apples okay? How many? Two be enough?"

The old woman gave a slight nod.

"And saltine crackers. I know you want a box."

Another quick nod.

Grandma looked in my direction. "George, Auntie Drusilla is going to need some snuff, also. How 'bout getting a jar of Garrett."

I got the snuff and brought it to the basket.

Auntie Hoosilla took it out of the basket, turned it over, and rubbed her fingers on the bottom of the jar. She set the jar beside the basket and slid it away with the back of her hand.

Grandma picked it up, looked at the bottom, then smiled at me. "This is a two-dot jar, George. Auntie prefers three dots." Each jar had one, two, three, or four dots on the bottom. Some people thought the dots represented the strength of the tobacco.

I took the offending jar back and looked until I found one with three dots on the bottom. I placed it in the basket and returned to the bleach. I hoped Auntie Hoosilla understood it was an honest mistake.

In a few minutes, Grandma placed all the groceries in a paper sack and walked with the woman to the front door. "Come back to see us, Auntie," she said.

Through the front window, I saw Auntie Hoosilla move away slowly down the road.

Suddenly, it occurred to me that I didn't hear the

cash register ring, and I had never seen an account book with Drusilla Cardamone's name on it.

I hurried over to the counter. "Grandma, she didn't pay," I said.

Grandma looked up at me over her reading glasses. "Yes, she did," she said. "She always pays."

Then she looked back to her figures.

After work, I ran home, thinking maybe Dog had returned. He hadn't.

I went on to the pond. Bennett and Esther were already there, sitting on the bank, lines in the water.

"I've already caught three," Esther said. "Bennett only has one, and it's a bit small. Definitely not a nickel fish."

Bennett made no response.

I told them all I could remember about Auntie Hoosilla. "I wonder what she looks like under that hood," I said. "I heard witches have red eyes."

"Carson Washington saw her once with the hood pulled back," Bennett said. "He said her face was the ugliest thing you ever saw, that she had this scraggly hair but was mostly bald like a man and her face was all twisted up from where the devil touched her, and that if you looked at it more than five seconds at a time you'd turn into a pillar of salt. He said the sheriff made her wear that hood just to keep people from dying when they looked at her."

"Hey!" came a loud voice from behind us. "Y'all caught anything?"

It was Winston and his friend from the sawmill, Jonathan Spears. They were walking down the path from Elizabeth's place.

Winston walked over to the wire stringer fastened to the edge of the bank and pulled it out of the water.

"Leave that alone," said Bennett.

Winston laughed. "There's nothing but puny fish here," he said. He put the stringer back in the water. "If y'all want to really catch some fish, you gonna have to go over to Vorhise's pond."

"I caught a five-pound bass there," said Jonathan. He was standing right behind Esther, his knees almost touching her. She ignored him.

"Yeah, sure," Bennett said skeptically.

"Last week we caught us eighty-five bream in one evening," said Winston. "Of course, there's a lunatic over there. You got to watch out for him 'cause he'll kill you. But there sure is some fish in that pond."

He reached down, picked up a rock, and tried to skip it across the surface of the water.

"Hey!" said Bennett. "Cut that out!"

Esther gave Winston a menacing look.

He laughed louder and picked up another rock, threw it, then pushed Bennett in the back of the head. "What you gonna do about it, punk?"

Bennett put his pole down and started to get up,

but Esther was already on her feet, turning at once toward Winston.

Winston and Jonathan both laughed and retreated.

"Leave us alone," she said, standing with both feet spread out and her hands knotted into fists at her side.

Winston scooped up a handful of small rocks and sprayed them into the air over the pond, then walked quickly away. Jonathan followed him.

I breathed a little easier. The mere presence of Winston was scary.

"I hate him," said Bennett. "And they ain't caught no eighty-five fish in one day."

Esther sat down again and picked up her pole. She didn't say anything.

A half hour passed without any of us getting a nibble.

Esther pulled her pole out of the water again, put on a fresh worm, and said, "Maybe we ought to go over there to Mr. Vorhise's and see if there really are some fish in that pond. What's eighty-five times five cents?"

Bennett jerked his head around to look at her. "You crazy? Didn't you hear what they said about that lunatic?"

"You know how Winston lies."

"I know. That's how come I think he's lying about the eighty-five fish. I think his ugly friend is lying about the bass, too."

Esther looked to the east in the direction of

Mr. Vorhise's land. "You've been over there, Bennett. Can you see the pond from his house?" I could hear the eagerness in her voice.

"I only went there once," said Bennett, "and I didn't get out of the back of the truck. Mr. Vorhise was just wanting to pick up something in his house. But I did see the kennels, and I bet those dogs could smell your stupid self a mile away. And I'm a lot more scared of them dogs than I am of any lunatic that probably don't exist anymore than them eighty-five fish."

"What about it, George?" she asked. "You want to go, don't you? It'll be exciting."

"Sure," I said, my voice a bit choked. I was slightly apprehensive, but it sounded like an adventure. "Sure," I said again, more forcefully, and at the same time wondered if Bennett noticed she'd called me George. I cleared my throat. "But maybe if I spoke to Grandma, she could ask Mr. Vorhise if we could—"

"Ha!" Bennett said. "Don't hold your breath! That man ain't never gave nothing to nobody but grief."

"You're just chicken," Esther said to him. "And you can just stay here and not catch any fish. George and I will go by ourselves, won't we, George." She looked at me and nodded as if to assure me.

"It's kind of late now, don't you think?" I said. "I mean, the sun's going down. It's going to be dark soon."

"Tomorrow then," said Esther, turning to walk away.

"We'll catch lots of fish. And if any lunatic shows up, I'll just mojo those dogs into attacking him instead of us."

After she left, Bennett said to me, "You don't really think she could control them dogs, do you?"

"Naw," I said, but, at the same time, I wasn't really quite sure.

Thirteen

The next morning I left the house just as the sun was coming up and walked to town to look for Dog. I looked in the yards and between the houses all along the road. Bennett said Dog could have gotten with a pack. But I didn't see two dogs together, much less a pack.

When I came home, Grandma said, "If it'll make you feel any better, I'll run an ad in the paper."

I told her I'd like that.

At lunch the next afternoon, Esther asked me in a hushed voice, "You didn't say anything to your grandmother, did you?"

"Why would you ask me that?" I said in a peeved voice.

She smiled. "I knew you wouldn't."

Bennett sighed. He still didn't want to go. I wasn't totally comfortable with the idea myself, but I did like the excitement of doing something so daring.

"We already got a place to fish," Bennett said. "One day I caught forty-five—"

"You ain't caught 'em lately," she interrupted, rising from the table and gathering up her plate and empty tea glass. "And if you're too chicken, George and I can go by ourselves."

Bennett glared at her but said nothing in reply.

"I'll meet y'all in back of the barn right after work," she said.

All during the rest of the day, my mouth felt very dry. I kept drinking water, but the chalky taste wouldn't go away. I remembered Bennett once said Mr. Vorhise let his dogs out to exercise. What if he decided to turn them loose while we were fishing at his pond? What if they attacked us?

I told Grandma I was meeting Bennett and Esther and ran to the house as soon as she closed the store. Esther was already at the barn, holding all three poles and a can of freshly dug red worms. Bennett arrived in a few minutes.

Esther led the way. Each of us carried a pole. Esther carried the can, and Bennett the wire stringer.

We took an old path, almost completely overgrown now, back to the road that ran down to the cabins. Esther didn't want to take a chance of her mother seeing us and wondering where we were going.

In a few minutes, we crossed the road and waded through waist-high field weeds till we reached the barbed wire that divided Grandma's land from

Mr. Vorhise's. I caught my shirt on the wire and tore it a little as I pulled free.

Esther moved quickly through the woods, her bare feet almost silent as she weaved in and through thickets of brambles and vines. Bennett and I hurried to keep up.

"How you even know where this pond is?" grumbled Bennett.

"I figure it's fed by the same creek that feeds our pond," she said.

For the first time I noticed off to the left a small, three-inch-deep and three-foot-wide stream. The stream snaked back and forth, and we had to jump across it again and again.

"I see it!" Esther said. "Right ahead."

Through the trees I could see the bright water reflecting the glare of the late afternoon sun. Esther began running, and we hurried after her.

We stood at the mouth of the stream where it flowed into the pond. The hardwoods thinned out on the left side, and a grove of pine trees fanned around a cove. On the right side there were no trees, only a hillside of tall grasses that sloped down to the water's edge. The dam was directly across from us.

Esther walked to the right. She stopped about half-way around and gazed out over the water. "Now, let's see if they were telling us the truth or not."

She baited her hook and set the can on the ground.

"I feel like I'm going to puke," Bennett said.

Esther chuckled. "George ain't scared, are you, George?"

I shook my head, took out a wriggling worm, and began threading it onto my hook. I didn't say anything because I was afraid my voice might squeak.

"Got one!" Esther said.

Her pole was bent almost double as she lifted an enormous bream out of the water.

Bennett hurried and baited his hook.

Within five seconds of dropping my line into the water, the cork was snatched under, and I felt a weight on my line like I'd never felt at Grandma's pond, even when I'd caught an occasional bass.

"Glory!" said Bennett, immediately lifting a fish out of the water.

We took the fish off the hooks and slid them onto the stringer and rebaited as fast as we could. It was always the same: we'd drop our lines into the water and *swoosh*, the corks would go underwater, then our poles would nearly bend in half as we lifted the fish out of the water to the bank. With every fish we landed, Esther repeated again how many each of us had caught and how much money each of us would receive.

Occasionally, a fish would swallow the hook down deep enough in its mouth that I had to use my Barlow knife to dislodge it. I left the knife open and beside the can of worms because Bennett and Esther needed it as well.

The sun had almost dropped behind the pine trees when, suddenly, I heard a noise. It sounded like someone running. Then it stopped.

I looked around, back up the hillside. Bennett turned to look at the same time.

"What's the matter?" asked Esther.

"What was that?" Bennett asked.

"What was what?"

"There's something up there in the grass," he said.

She sneered. "Sure," she said. "It's just your lunatic. Maybe he's got a couple of dogs with him." She winked at me to let me know she knew I wasn't afraid, even if her brother was.

I dropped my eyes back to the water. Somehow, I could feel that there really was someone there. And I knew whoever it was, was looking at us.

Fourteen

The next day as soon as she came into the store, Elizabeth tied on her apron and said to Grandma, "My heavens, I ain't never seen such a mess of fish as them childrens brought home last night. Took me 'most an hour to clean them, Miss Tilly."

"Thirty-two is the figure George gave me," said Grandma.

"Seemed like sixty-two," Elizabeth said with a laugh.

Esther had caught sixteen, Bennett six, and me ten. Yesterday, when I reported our totals to Grandma, she lined off three columns in a spiral notebook and wrote each of our names at the top of a column. "I'll keep a running record of who catches how many and pay up just before homecoming," she said.

I avoided any unnecessary comments about the afternoon because I didn't want to invite questions. I knew Grandma and Elizabeth assumed we'd caught the fish at our pond, and I sure didn't want to have to lie about it. Grandma could always tell just by just looking at my face whether I was lying or not.

At lunch, Esther was excited. "Maybe we can catch forty," she said. "Maybe fifty."

"Mama's going to get tired of cleaning all them fish," Bennett said.

"Stop being so chicken," she said to him. "You don't hear George whimpering about no dogs or lunatics, do you?"

After work we went again. This time, knowing where the pond was, we took a more direct route through the woods, saving time for fishing before the sun set. Bennett carried two stringers. Esther had dug up twice as many worms as we'd had the day before.

Just as had happened the previous afternoon, the fish tore after the worms, and we pulled them in one after another.

As I was on one knee rinsing my hands in the water after putting a fish on a stringer, I glanced up the hillside and saw someone. More precisely I saw a head. A white person with blond hair. My heart jumped.

Slowly I stepped beside Esther.

"There is someone on the hillside watching us," I said. I didn't say it was the lunatic. I didn't have to.

Esther turned around carefully, ever so slowly.

"Yes," she said softly. "He doesn't look so bad. I don't even think he's a grown man."

"I'm leaving," said Bennett.

"Don't move," she said. "I'm taking care of this."

She waved.

The boy waved back.

Esther waved again, and he waved again also.

She took a few steps toward the hillside, paused, and waved. He waved. She took a few more steps in his direction and waved once more.

Bennett and I didn't move. It occurred to me watching Esther carefully make her way up the hillside that there was probably nothing in the world that Esther was afraid of. If she had told me she was going to walk into a den of lions, I would not have doubted for one moment that she would.

Before long, she reached the place near the summit where the boy was. She was talking to him, but I couldn't hear what she was saying.

He stood up. He was even taller than Esther, shirtless and wearing a pair of baggy khakis. She talked with him a little longer, then took him by the hand and walked with him back down the bank.

"This is Jimmy," she said. "He's our friend."

Up close I could see that he was even bigger than Winston and probably about the same age. He grinned a lopsided grin at us. "I'm Jimmy," he said, pointing to his chest.

"We're catching fish, Jimmy," Esther said. "You want to catch fish?"

He nodded and kept grinning.

She put the pole in his hands, still holding it herself, and swung the line back out into the water. A bream struck immediately, and together they pulled it in. Jimmy squealed and laughed.

Just as they landed their fourth fish together, a bell sounded in the distance, a dinner bell.

Jimmy looked up the hillside at once, turned to grin at Esther, then left at a half trot.

"Good-bye, Jimmy," she called after him.

After he disappeared over the hill, she turned to Bennett. "Some lunatic," she said.

Bennett gave a worried look in the direction Jimmy had gone. "He's probably gonna tell his father now, and he's gonna turn them dogs loose."

Esther chuckled and said, "How many fish we caught already? More than thirty-two?"

Grandma made tomato sandwiches for supper and poured me and herself each a glass of buttermilk. "How many fish tonight?" she asked as I sat down.

"Forty-one," I said.

She chuckled and picked up the spiral notebook to enter the figures.

I finished my first sandwich and reached for a second. "What's Mr. Vorhise's family like?" I asked, wanting to know more about the boy Jimmy but also knowing I had to be careful not to give away anything about going to the pond.

She wiped her mouth with her napkin. "His wife's name is Calley. She stays at the house mostly. Mr. Vorhise does the shopping. I don't know when I saw her last. I suspect she spends a lot of her time taking care of Jimmy."

"That's their son?" I asked, feigning ignorance.

"Yes, their only child. I've only seen him once. I went over with a pie right after they moved back a few years ago. He's a bit slow."

"Slow?"

"A bit."

"Do you like Mr. Vorhise?"

She gave me a surprised look. "What kind of question is that? Of course, I like him. I like everybody. I will admit he's always been a little peculiar, but he's not had an easy life. His family didn't have much, and he had to drop out of school and go to work. Would have graduated with your mother otherwise. Then he went into the Navy. I don't know what happened there. They let him go, and then he went to Mississippi." She wiped her mouth again. "And if he wasn't taking care of my cows, I'd have to get rid of them all, and I can't do that just yet. I figure in a couple of years maybe Bennett will be grown enough to handle them. He says he wants to be a farmer like his father was."

"Is Jimmy dangerous?"

"Dangerous? I wouldn't think so."

"How come they don't take him anyplace?"

"I suppose they want to protect him. They don't want people making fun of him. You know how people can act sometimes. You sure are full of questions. Why are you thinking about Mr. Vorhise?"

"Just curious," I said. I didn't ask anything else. That was enough for now. My main worry at the moment was whether or not Jimmy was too slow to tell his father we'd been at the pond. Mr. Vorhise was definitely a man I wouldn't want coming after me for stealing some of his fish.

Fifteen

The next afternoon as we followed the stream once again to the pond, Bennett said, "There's no way they caught eighty-five fish before dark. Winston was lying. Or else they came on a Saturday and had more time."

Esther didn't answer him but pressed on until we were once again on the bank. Again the fish were biting but not quite as readily as the day before. We moved a short ways farther around the pond and found a spot were they were more active.

Jimmy returned, standing for a few minutes at the top of the hillside. Esther waved and called to him to come on down. Finally, he came.

In his hand he held a bunch of wild flowers, the soft lavender ones that look like morning glories, and several kinds of white flowers, even a few angel flowers. He held them out to Esther.

"How sweet," she said. "I bet you pick flowers for your mother, don't you?"

He grinned and nodded.

She set the flowers beside the can of worms and let Jimmy help her fish. He laughed every time they landed one.

We only caught thirty-eight bream, but also a mud cat and a nice-sized bass.

That was our last big catch. In the following days the fish were either almost all gone or—and Esther said she knew this for a fact—the moon was affecting their hunger.

Jimmy brought Esther flowers every day. Since the fish weren't biting, he didn't stand beside her holding onto the pole but sat on the bank a few feet from her like a puppy dog, a joyous look on his face. I wondered if he'd ever seen a girl before.

He always left when the dinner bell rang.

The following Tuesday we fished for over half an hour without getting a nibble. Esther looked across the pond at the grove of pine trees around a shaded cove. "You know," she said, "if I was a fish, I would love to lay around over there. I'd be in the shade and could look up at the pretty pines. Let's try over there."

She picked up the day's bunch of wild flowers and said to me, "Bring the worms." Then, holding the pole and the flowers in the same hand, she reached out her other hand to Jimmy. "Come on, you handsome man. Let's find those fish."

She led the way, walking to the dam, holding Jimmy's hand, with me and Bennett following.

As soon as she reached the dam, however, Jimmy stopped and pulled back. "No!" he said. "No, no."

"Come on, Jimmy," she said, pulling at his hand.

His face was twisted with panic. "No, no, no!" he yelled, now pulling on her hand with both of his.

He was stronger than Esther, and she almost slipped down. Quickly she jerked her hand out of his hand. "All right," she said. "You don't have to come."

He started crying. "No, no, no!"

Bennett and I walked past him, following Esther across the dam toward the pines. I looked back and saw him running away up the hillside. He disappeared over the top.

"What was that all about?" I asked.

"Who knows?" she said.

We reached the pines and dropped our lines into the water.

Swoosh! All three corks disappeared at the same time. We pulled in fish and rebaited as quick as we could. Both wire stringers were filling up fast.

We were so intent on fishing that we didn't see them coming over the hillside. We heard Jimmy wailing and looked up. He was standing at the top of the hill with his hands on the sides of his face, and Mr. Vorhise was already down the hill and running along the bank toward us. He had a shotgun in his hands.

Esther threw down her pole and darted off in the opposite direction from Mr. Vorhise and Jimmy.

Bennett and I did the same, jumping over low vines and smashing through bushes and weaving around trees. Low limbs lashed across my face, but I stayed right behind Esther.

Boom! sounded the gun and on we ran. I didn't know whether Mr. Vorhise was shooting at us or into the air, and it didn't make any difference. I couldn't have been more terrified.

"Stop!" Mr. Vorhise yelled. "Come back here!"

Esther outran us immediately, and soon I wasn't even sure which way she'd gone.

Boom!

I ran harder, pumping my legs as fast as I could, falling and sliding face first into the moist leaves under the heavy canopy of hardwoods, scrambling to my feet, and plunging on again.

I was breathing hard, desperately breathing, before I was halfway through the woods, but on I ran. Bennett was right behind me. I expected at any moment one of Mr. Vorhise's fighting dogs to lunge upon me from behind. I hadn't seen a dog, but that didn't mean there might not be one.

We reached the barbed-wire boundary fence, scooted under it, and ran to the road. Esther was waiting for us. We looked in each other's faces. No one had to say it. We were sick with fear, not only from being chased by Mr. Vorhise, but about what would happen if Grandma and Elizabeth found out what we'd done.

"He couldn't . . . ," said Esther, gasping, ". . . couldn't have known who we were."

"He knows me," said Bennett.

"And me," I said. I was bent over, holding onto my knees.

We walked back down the road toward the cabins.

I rubbed my hand on my pants pocket and stopped dead in my tracks. I felt my stomach rise up toward my throat. "My knife . . . ," I said. "I left my knife back there."

"Forget it," Bennett said.

"No," I said. "I have to go back."

"Then go back," he said. "I'm going home." He looked like he was going to cry.

Esther gazed back in the direction we'd just come. She didn't say anything for a while. Then she looked at me. "Okay," she said. "He's probably already gone back to his house by now. Let's go get it."

Sixteen

It was dusk as we moved quietly through the woods back toward the pond. Esther walked ahead, and I followed.

We stopped just at the edge of the stream's mouth and looked. Jimmy was standing on the bank near the dam. He was still wailing and holding the sides of his face.

"Go on home," came the voice of his father from the pine grove. "I'll be along directly."

But the boy didn't move. He wrung his hands and moaned and looked toward his father.

Esther and I squatted behind a huckleberry bush. I caught a glimpse of Mr. Vorhise moving around in the pines. I was hardly breathing.

"What's he doing?" I whispered to Esther.

She shook her head.

I didn't see any sign of a dog.

Finally, he walked out of the pines and back across the dam. With one hand he held the shotgun at his side.

"It's all right," he said to Jimmy. "There's nothing to be afraid of."

When he reached the boy, he took his hand, and together they walked up the hillside and disappeared over the top.

"Wait just a minute longer," Esther whispered. "Just to make sure he's not coming back."

We waited. That minute seemed like an hour. Then she said, "I'll stay here and watch," she said. "You go back through these trees to the pines and get your knife. I'll keep a look out. If he comes back over the hill, I'll whistle."

I nodded.

"And get the poles," she said.

I hurried along the edge of the water, hoping, now that darkness was gathering, I wouldn't be seen. The poles were on the bank where we'd thrown them. The can of worms was still in place. But the knife was gone. I searched all around the area but didn't see it.

I gathered up the poles, left the can, and returned to Esther.

"It was gone," I said.

We moved back through the woods to the road. Bennett was waiting. It was dark now.

We washed up at the pump in back of their cabin. Bennett kept whimpering softly.

Esther told him to shut up.

I returned to Grandma's and took a deep breath just before I went in through the back door, determined at all costs to avoid looking at her. I knew she'd see into my heart and know everything. I had no idea how long it would be before she noticed I wasn't using my Barlow knife.

"That you, George?" Grandma called out from the front room.

"Yessum," I said, looking down at my shirt. In the light I could see how dirty it was. I started unbuttoning it.

"Come, George," she called. "We have a visitor."

I caught my breath. I knew, even before she said anything else, who it was.

"Mr. Vorhise is here," she said. "Come in here, please."

Seventeen

Mr. Vorhise was sitting on the edge of an easy chair, his elbows on his knees and his hat in his hands. He did not look up at me when I walked in. His face was very grim.

Grandma patted the place beside her on the couch, gesturing for me to sit down. I did.

"Now," she said to me, "do you want to tell me what this is all about?"

"We were . . . ," I began, but my voice choked. I swallowed and tried again. "We were fishing," I managed. My voice was quivering.

"On Mr. Vorhise's property?"

I nodded, my head down.

"I can't be responsible for somebody else's children running around on my land," he said. "I mean, what if one of them was to drown? But the main thing is I can't have people frightening my Jimmy. He's on his bed in the house right now curled up like a baby. There ain't no call for that."

"I thoroughly understand," Grandma said. "And I

can assure you it will never happen again, can't I, George?"

"Yessum," I mumbled.

"And I'll speak to Elizabeth about Bennett and Esther," she continued, looking at Mr. Vorhise. "There won't be any need for you to bring it up." I could tell by the firmness in her tone that she meant for him not to carry the matter any further with the Garrison family. She looked at me. "Now, George, do you have something to say to Mr. Vorhise?"

I cleared my throat. "I'm sorry," I said.

He stood up, reached into his trouser pocket, and took out my knife. Without a word, he held it out to me. I took it and said thank you.

He turned to go.

"Excuse me, sir," I quickly said.

He looked back at me, his brow knitted.

"My dog is gone," I said. "You wouldn't have seen my dog, would you?"

He shook his head slowly. "It's a bad thing to lose a dog," he said. "If I see him, I'll bring him over."

Then he was gone.

"Go take a bath," Grandma said to me. "I'm going down to Elizabeth's. I'll be back shortly."

Grandma said nothing else about it, not that night or the next morning.

"Listen to me," Esther said at lunch, glancing

toward the back door to be sure no one was standing there. "I kept thinking about this all night."

"So did I," Bennett said. "I thought maybe he'd kill me when I came to work this morning, but Mr. Vorhise didn't say a word."

"No," she said. "There's something very peculiar here. I don't know what it is, but I think it's peculiar. Why would Jimmy have acted like that? I mean, every day we've been going there and every day he was just as happy as punch. Then, suddenly, he starts all that whooping. How come?"

"He's not all there," I said, tapping the side of my head.

"He understands a lot more than you think," she said. "No, there's something about that pine grove."

"Forget it," said Bennett. "I don't even want to talk about it anymore."

"Jimmy was all right as long as we were fishing on the south side of the pond. And he was all right when we moved back and forth all along the bank. He was all right when we first started onto the dam. It was only when he realized we were going to the pines that he got upset." She paused and gave a knowing nod. "And then later when George and I went back, Mr. Vorhise was still walking around in the pines. We were long gone. He knew that. He'd had plenty of time to walk over and see where we'd been fishing and then leave. Why was he still there?" She looked at me, as if expecting an answer.

I shook my head and took a mouthful of black-eyed peas. I didn't have any idea where she was going with this.

"I think Mr. Vorhise has somehow scared Jimmy real bad about the place where the pines are," she continued. "He obviously doesn't want his boy messing around over there. Jimmy seems to wander around wherever he wants otherwise. All he has to do is listen out for the dinner bell."

Bennett was scowling. "What are you saying?"

"I'm saying there is some reason Jimmy is scared of going to the pines. And he is so scared of that place that he didn't want us to go either. That's why he ran off and got his father. And then Mr. Vorhise comes with a shotgun." She looked at me. "Did you tell Miss Tilly he shot at us with a shotgun?"

I shook my head.

"Well, she knows now. I told Mama. She got so upset about that, she couldn't even whup us."

"She don't whup us no more anyways," said Bennett. "Not me, leastways."

"And why was Mr. Vorhise still there when we got back, George? I'll tell you why. He was looking all around. He was checking something out. That's what I think."

"What I think is that you're nuts," said Bennett.

She turned to him. "And who was his grandfather?"

Bennett shook his head. "What has any of that got to do with anything?"

"Remember, I told you he was one of the bank-robbing Chism brothers."

Both Bennett and I stared at her. I stopped chewing.

She nodded knowingly. "I'll tell you what I think," she said. "I think Mr. Vorhise has got his granddaddy's money buried out there in those pines. That's how come he has to keep everybody away, including his own son. No telling how much money is there. Maybe it's not just his granddaddy's share, but all that money that was stolen and never recovered."

"So what?" asked Bennett.

"So maybe we ought to go check it out."

"What!" he exclaimed. He looked at me. "Didn't I tell you she was nuts?"

"It's not Mr. Vorhise's money," she said. "It belonged to the bank. And like I've told you, sand brains, banks are insured. That means they get paid for what they lose. So that money is money for anybody's taking."

"I . . . I promised Grandma I'd stay off Mr. Vorhise's land," I said.

"Did you?" she asked, looking at me and raising one eyebrow. "Did you really?"

I nodded.

"You said, 'I promise not to go back onto Mr. Vorhise's land'?"

"Well . . . not exactly in those words."

"Then you didn't really promise. Think about it, George. You'll have enough money for one of those brand new motorcycles. What are they called?"

"Harley-Davidsons."

"Right. And what are you going to do with the money, Bennett?"

"I'm not going to do nothing, because I ain't going back there never."

I laid down my fork. Suddenly, I wasn't hungry at all. I knew somehow that if Esther Garrison decided she was really going to go back to that pond that I would go with her. From that moment, a knot that wouldn't go away sprang up in the middle of my chest.

Eighteen

Esther talked about little else but going back to the pines at Mr. Vorhise's pond and finding the bank robbers' money. She wanted to know how much money they'd taken, so she went to the colored folks' library— a small, one-room brick building in town beside the colored cafe—to search back through old newspapers to find information on the robberies. The library had newspapers dating back only to 1945.

She had me go to the white library to see what I could find. The librarian told me the old library burned down in 1926, and all the books and newspapers were destroyed. Besides, she said, the *Pontola County Times* didn't start up until the beginning of World War II. Maybe the Demopolis library might have something.

Esther figured there had to be at least ten thousand dollars buried in the pine grove. Where she got this figure I have no idea.

The following Tuesday, exactly one week since the incident at Mr. Vorhise's pond, Esther, Bennett, and I were sitting on Grandma's back porch. We kept our voices low as we talked.

"We could turn it all over to the insurance company," Esther said. "They'd give us the reward. I mean, to them the ten thousand dollars is gone. It might as well be burned up. So maybe they'd give us 10 percent. A thousand dollars. How much is that a piece, George?"

I tried dividing in my head, but before I could answer, she said, "It's $333.33 each. Except one of us would get thirty-four cents. We'd let George have the thirty-four cents. Is that all right with you, Bennett?"

He groaned.

She smiled with confidence. "We'll have to go at night. The darker the better. You have a flashlight, George?"

"Grandma has one in the kitchen."

"You'll have to borrow it. We got a shovel. What else do we need?"

The knot in my chest was throbbing.

She nodded her head firmly. "We can be in and out in minutes. He'll never even know we were there."

"When are you thinking of doing this?" I asked.

She looked surprised. "Why, tonight, of course. After supper, after it gets full dark." She gave a little giggle and winked at me. "I bet you don't have this much fun in Mobile, do you, George?"

I told Grandma we were going to spot deer. That was why I needed the flashlight. Spotting deer was Esther's idea. She said my grandfather and her father used to do that together some. Both of them liked to hunt, and during the off-season they wanted to know where the deer were feeding and where they bedded down at night. They would walk around the fields and the edges of the woods shining a flashlight and looking for deer.

Esther said she went with them once. She was about nine. Granddaddy would shine the beam of light around until a deer's eyes lit up, reflecting the light. And the deer wouldn't move, she said, but would be hypnotized by the light.

Grandma seemed so pleased that I wanted to spot deer that I felt all the more guilty for telling her a story. As I followed the path to the Garrisons', I told myself that maybe we would see some deer and then it wouldn't be a complete lie.

There was a full moon, and it lit our way. Walking on the road and on the path we'd worn through the tall grass was easy. Walking in the dark woods, however, was another matter. But Esther didn't want to turn on the flashlight until we absolutely had to. Each of us took turns tripping on vines and falling. Finally, Esther turned on the flashlight, and Bennett and I stayed close behind her. It was slow going.

"Wait," said Bennett right after we crossed the second little creek. "I heard something."

Esther snorted. "There's lots of 'somethings' in the woods," she said. "Thousands of them."

"No," he said, looking behind us. "This sounded like somebody walking."

The three of us stood perfectly still for a moment. Everything was still.

"Probably a squirrel or a possum," said Esther, continuing on.

As we walked, I listened, and at least twice I heard what I very definitely thought were footsteps. Footsteps like someone following us.

We arrived at the pond. The moon was reflected in the still water. We made our way to the pine grove.

"How in the world are we supposed to know where to dig?" asked Bennett.

Esther walked back and forth with the flashlight, shining the oval beam of light all around. She found what she took to be a small mound of earth.

"Here," she said. "Dig."

She held the light, and Bennett began digging. The ground was soft, and he was down to the one-foot level quickly. Nothing but worms and small roots.

"Cover it up," she said, "We need to try someplace else."

He refilled the hole, and we stomped the dirt flat.

There was a log on the ground—not a big log, but more like a small tree with broken branches. A fallen tree. Esther walked around it with the light, carefully looking at the ground all around the tree.

She looked up at us. "No stump," she said.

"What?" I asked.

"No stump. This tree was hauled over here from someplace else." She swept her light around the trees behind us. "And look at it. This ain't a pine."

Bennett and I pulled the tree to one side.

Again she held the light, and Bennett started digging. Almost immediately the blade of the shovel turned over something in the dirt. It looked like a piece of rotten blanket.

Esther bent down and pulled at it. The piece she was holding tore as easily as wet paper.

Bennett turned another shovelful of dirt. A tin can.

"See," he said. "This is just where some old house was."

Suddenly, there was a sound. All three of us froze. It was a dog. Or dogs. Several. Barking madly.

Bennett turned and dashed away, back the way we'd come.

"Grab the shovel," Esther said to me.

I did, and she moved on ahead of me, flicking off the flashlight. I followed.

The barking was louder, closer.

We ran and stumbled and fell, crawled and rose again to run and fall and rise again.

Once, I tripped on a root or vine or something and sprawled headfirst into the moist leaves. Esther and Bennett were moving on ahead of me. I pushed myself to my feet and right in front of me was a something—I thought it was a tree at first—that suddenly moved to the side and slipped into the darkness of trees and brambles.

I hurried on after Bennett and Esther, and, as I ran, I realized that what I had seen back there was a person, was, in fact, Auntie Hoosilla.

Nineteen

We reached the road again and stopped. All three of us struggled to catch our breath. The dogs had come no closer. They weren't as loud now and seemed to have settled down.

"Fool face," said Esther to Bennett. "Why did you run? They weren't after us."

"She was there," I said.

"Who?" asked Esther.

"Auntie Hoosilla."

Esther gave me a puzzled glance but made no comment. Then she looked back toward Vorhise's land. "I want to go again," she said.

Neither Bennett nor I replied. We both started walking toward home. Esther could go back whenever she wanted to, but it would definitely not be with me. And I knew it wouldn't be with Bennett, either. As far as we were concerned, Esther could have the ten thousand dollars or the one-thousand-dollar reward or whatever. We were never ever in a million years under any circumstances whatsoever going back to that pond.

The following Saturday, Winston and his buddy

Jonathan Spears came into the store. Winston had a big smile on his face.

"I got me a car," he announced to his mother. "And I wants you to come go for a ride."

"Car?" she asked, her eyes widening with disbelief. "Where'd you get a car?"

"I bought it, Mama," he said. "Got the bill of sale right here." He took a piece of paper out of his pocket and handed it to her. "And I'm gonna take you wherever you wants to go."

She looked at it. "And where'd you get ninety-five dollars?"

He smiled again. "I been putting aside a dollar here and a dollar there," he said, leading us all back through the store and outside. "And this morning me and Jonathan got a ride with Roe Blanchard up to Demopolis, and I seen this car on a car lot. I knew it was mine. And here it is."

Parked beside the gas pump was a dark green automobile, a 1939 four-door Dodge. The windshield was cracked, and the rear passenger-side door was caved in slightly. Other than that, it wasn't bad looking.

I noticed Jonathan was standing beside Esther in front of the car. He was saying something to her, speaking low. She wasn't paying him any attention.

Winston held the back door open and bowed regally to Elizabeth. "At your service, my lady," he said.

She laughed and shook her head. "No. Not now. I

gots too much work to do. Maybe you can take us all to church tomorrow."

Winston didn't reply. He hadn't been to church since Staple left.

"Let's go," he said to Jonathan, getting into the car. He tilted his cap in a jaunty manner.

"Come on," Jonathan said to Esther. He was holding open the passenger door. "You know you want to."

There was a look in her eyes I'd seen so often when something exciting and different came her way. She gave a shrug and said, "Okay."

"Y'all be careful," said Elizabeth.

Esther got in, and they left.

Grandma and Elizabeth went back inside the store, and Bennett and I watched till the car disappeared around the bend in the road.

Bennett shook his head. "You ain't gonna catch me riding in that thing with him," he said. "He could get you killed sure 'nough."

Elizabeth was through for the day, and Bennett didn't have to work on Saturday afternoons. They went home together.

I had to go back to work. Grandma had a lot of empty cardboard boxes she wanted me to break down and burn in the rubbish pit out behind the store.

The rest of the afternoon passed quickly. I got all the trash burned and went through the potato bin and threw away any potatoes that were getting spoiled. I did the same with the bananas, apples, and pears and was emptying the bottle caps from the opener attached to the side of the drink box when the front screen door flew open and slammed against the wall.

Bennett stood in the doorway. His eyes were wide with fear. "Miss Tilly!" he cried out. "There's been a bad accident. Mama wants you to come right away."

Twenty

Grandma told me to lock up the back door and turn off the lights. She snatched all the money out of the cash register and shoved the money into her purse. I turned the sign on the door around to "CLOSED," and we both stepped outside. She locked the door, and the three of us hurried toward Grandma's. I'd never seen Grandma walk so fast.

Bennett told us that a man came by their house and said Winston had been in a wreck. "Mama sent me to get you," he continued. "The man say they been taken to the clinic at Toshkey."

Toshkey was about twenty miles northwest of Obadiah on the other side of the Tombigbee River.

Elizabeth was standing in the front yard of Grandma's house. "Oh, Miss Tilly," she cried. "My babies. My babies."

"Let's go get the car," said Grandma.

We got into the car, me in front beside Grandma, and Elizabeth and Bennett in back. Grandma drove carefully, staying just within the speed limit. Elizabeth cried softly all the way.

The Toshkey Clinic was a small white building beside the city hall. A receptionist ushered us into the colored waiting room, a tiny room with an entry door on the side of the building. Esther and Winston were sitting in chairs opposite each other.

Esther rose at once and hugged her mother. Her left eye was badly swollen, and she had a white bandage on her forehead.

Winston sat with a scowl on his face. His right arm was in a sling.

"He got a dislocated shoulder," the nurse explained to Elizabeth and Grandma. "The doctor got it back in okay. The other boy was taken to Demopolis. They have a colored unit at their hospital. We don't have one here."

She said that Jonathan had several injuries, including a broken arm, broken leg, and severe facial cuts. The car went off the road and crashed against a tree on his side.

On the ride back to Obadiah no one said anything except Elizabeth. She sat in back between Esther and Winston and kept humming and whispering, "Thank you, Jesus," every once in a while.

Bennett sat between me and Grandma.

By the time we got home it was dark. Grandma parked in the garage, and we all got out. Winston immediately walked away, back to the road and not toward their house.

"Where you going, son?" Elizabeth called after him.

"Town," he said without looking back.

"Why don't you just come on home with us now," she said. There was a pleading in her voice.

Winston didn't answer. He didn't even look back.

Grandma put her arm around Elizabeth. "Come on inside," she said. "Let's have some coffee."

"I'm just so thankful they ain't hurt no worse," said Elizabeth as they walked toward the house.

"What happened?" Bennett asked Esther. We were standing in the backyard. The stars were bright.

"That fool could have got us all killed," Esther said, anger bristling in every word. "Next thing I know he and Jonathan are passing a liquor bottle back and forth. I told them to let me out, just let me out and I'd walk home."

She made an exasperated sigh, then continued. "But Winston kept laughing and speeding and weaving all over the road. And Jonathan was trying to get me to drink that liquor, and he was pushing that bottle in my face. Next thing I know we went over that river bridge and around a curve and off the road and hit that tree." She shook her head slowly. "I crawled over Winston and got out. He and Jonathan were just moaning away. I crawled back onto the road and got a car to stop. Two white men in a truck took us to that clinic."

She started walking toward the lane that led to her and Bennett's place. We followed.

When we reached their cabin, Bennett went around back to the outhouse.

Esther and I were standing in the middle of the lane. She looked up at the moon. "I was so mad," she said. "I was furious. I mean, right after it happened and I was trying to crawl over Winston to get out. I was crying and yelling at him. I told him if I died and couldn't go on to high school, I'd kill him. That's how mad I was."

I started to tell her how glad I was she wasn't killed or even hurt bad. But I didn't. I figured that might make her mad, too.

Twenty-One

Near the end of the noon hour on Monday, Mr. Avery Mayes, the owner of the sawmill Winston and Jonathan worked at, came into the store. He wore a yellow bow tie and a light gray cotton suit. He didn't look very happy.

"I need to speak with Elizabeth Garrison," he said to Grandma.

Grandma took him into the kitchen where Elizabeth and Esther were working. I had just cleaned a table and was carrying the tray to the sink.

"Where is Winston?" Mr. Mayes said to Elizabeth.

She explained about the wreck and that Winston had a separated shoulder and might have to be off a few days.

"Ain't no need for him to come back," he said. "He's fired. He stole ninety-five dollars from me, and I want it back right now."

"What?" said Elizabeth. She stood there holding a plate in one hand and the serving spoon to the mashed potatoes in the other. Her eyes got very wide.

"He stole my money. Friday evening we came up

short ninety-five dollars, and this morning I questioned everybody. We got witnesses who saw him go into the office when nobody else was in there."

Grandma crossed her arms. "Now, Avery," she said slowly. "Did any of these witnesses actually see him take the money?"

"Come on, Tilly." His anger was flaring up. "I got boys there who say he went to Demopolis Saturday and bought himself a car for ninety-five dollars. I want that money back. I don't want any rattletrap car, either."

Elizabeth's mouth trembled, but she didn't say anything.

"Let me put it like this," Mr. Mayes said. "If I don't get that ninety-five dollars back by tomorrow morning, I'm going to the sheriff and having him arrested. They'll send him to prison. And I'll do it. I'll be at the office by seven o'clock. If I don't have my ninety-five dollars by eight, I'm going to the sheriff."

He turned around and left.

Elizabeth looked helplessly at Grandma. Grandma walked over to her and took the plate and spoon out of her hand and held her hands. "Everything's going to be all right," she said.

"They gonna send him to prison," Elizabeth said in disbelief. "They gonna send my baby to prison." She was beginning to cry.

Bennett had just walked through the door.

Grandma put an arm around Elizabeth. "Let's step out onto the back porch for a moment," she said. She looked at me. "George, you take care of the customers. Bennett, you wash up and lend your sister a hand serving."

Bennett looked questioningly at me. "What's going on?"

I waited until Grandma and Elizabeth were outside, then told him.

Esther gave a snort. "As far as I'm concerned, they can put his sorry self at the bottom of the jail," she said.

"Where's Mama gonna get ninety-five dollars?" Bennett asked.

"How many times that boy been in trouble anyways?" Esther said, placing a filled plate on the serving board and reaching for another one. "Maybe in prison they can knock some sense into his ugly head."

I didn't like Winston—never had—and didn't care one way or the other if he went to prison. But at the same time, as I walked out of the kitchen with a pitcher of tea, I had a sinking feeling that the rest of us were going to get sucked into his troubles.

Twenty-Two

After work I walked down to the Garrisons' place. Esther and Bennett were sitting on the porch in the shade. From within the house came the sounds of loud moans from Elizabeth.

Esther sighed. "I don't know why she's carrying on like this. I mean, I've been knowing since I was old enough to know anything that they were going to send that boy to jail one day. It was bound to happen."

Elizabeth let out an especially loud cry and said something. All I could make out was, "My baby! My baby!"

Bennett gave a worried look at the front door. "I've never seen her like this," he said. "She's been in her room crying all afternoon. She ain't hardly stopped for one minute. She just lays there in bed and cries."

"Where's Winston?" I asked.

"Who cares?" said Esther.

"Probably at the pool hall," said Bennett. "He stays there more than he stays here."

"He's my first born, Lord!" came the cry. "Have mercy, please, sir! Let me die, Lord, but save my child!"

Bennett stood up and walked down the steps and stood in the road. "I can't stay here and listen to this," he said, kicking at a rock.

Esther groaned.

I decided to head home.

Grandma seemed to think the same way as Esther. "To be honest with you," she said at supper, "I think maybe prison may be the best thing that could be done for that boy. Maybe it'd finally get him straightened out."

I told her how Elizabeth was carrying on.

She took a long drink of her buttermilk, then said, "I can't tell you how it grieves me to see her suffer. We all feel that way about our children. I don't know how many bottles of tears I shed over your uncle Matthew. I tell you if he hadn't joined the merchant marines, I don't know what would have become of that boy."

"Where is Elizabeth going to get ninety-five dollars?"

Grandma shook her head. "I've never told Elizabeth this, but he's stolen from me, too. Several times. And besides that, I sure can't afford to give her that much money. It all just breaks my heart. For Elizabeth herself, I'd go to the bank and borrow anything she needed. I mean, if it was for her. But not for that Winston. No, sir. He's had too many extra chances."

As I continued to eat, I thought about Elizabeth asking God to let her die. I wondered if God ever made swaps like that.

Twenty-Three

The next morning I was in front of the store picking up litter when Elizabeth arrived. "Good morning, George," she said. She was beaming.

She walked past me, stepped up onto the porch, and went inside. She was humming a song. I followed her inside, put the sack of litter in the garbage, and paused as Elizabeth stopped at the counter to speak to Grandma.

"God is good," Elizabeth said. "He heard my cries."

"And?" asked Grandma.

"Everything is going to be all right, yes it is. It's all taken care of."

She went on into the kitchen.

Grandma gave me a questioning look. I shook my head and I went on with my work.

Later, when I went into the kitchen to wash my hands before setting the tables, I saw Elizabeth peeling potatoes. She was singing softly one of her church songs.

At eleven o'clock, Esther arrived. I was refilling the napkin holders at the tables and looked up as she walked by. She was wearing a much smaller bandage over the cut on her forehead, and the swelling over her eye seemed to have gone down.

The thing that struck me, though, was her eyes. They were puffy and red like she'd been crying.

During the middle of lunch I brought a stack of dirty dishes to the sink in the kitchen. Elizabeth and Esther were standing side by side, serving plates. Elizabeth was humming.

"Please," Esther said through her teeth. "I think I'm going to scream if you don't stop all that singing and humming."

"I'm just praising the good Lord, Esther," Elizabeth said.

"Do you mind doing it to yourself?" snapped Esther.

Bennett walked in just as the last customers were leaving. He nodded at me but didn't say anything.

Esther left the store without eating.

When Bennett and I were seated at the table, I said, "What happened?"

He hesitated a moment, broke his roll in half, and looked up at me. "Mama was able to take care of it," he said.

"How?"

"At seven o'clock this morning she walked down to the sawmill and stood in front of Mr. Mayes's desk and counted out $89.38 on his desk. It was mostly in one-dollar bills. There might have been maybe two five-dollar bills. And she counted it out and swore to him upon her heart that she would get the rest if he could just give her a little more time. That's exactly the way she told it to me when she got home."

"But . . . where . . . ?"

"Esther gave her the money."

"Esther?" I asked, not believing what he was saying.

He shook his head as if he couldn't believe it either. "All I know I was trying to get to sleep last night, and Mama was still moaning. Then I heard her and Esther talking. Then Mama started squealing and laughing and shouting glories. That went on for a long time. Finally, she quit. This morning Esther had one of those looks like she's going to slap your face if you speak to her, so I just stayed out of her way."

Later I asked Grandma if Elizabeth had told her what happened. She said she had, and that she also said that as soon as she got Mr. Mayes paid off she was going to start helping Esther save up her school money again, that Esther would have to wait a year to go off to school, but she was young and had plenty of time. The main thing right now was that Mr. Mayes wasn't going to the sheriff.

After work I went down to the Garrison place. Elizabeth said Bennett had to work late and wasn't home yet, and that Esther was around somewhere. I walked up the lane past the other cabins and on to the place where we'd cut a path through the tall grass to the woods when we went to Mr. Vorhise's pond. The thought crossed my mind that she might have decided to go back there again to try to find the money.

But it was still daylight. She wouldn't go till after dark.

The sun was blazing, and my shirt was sticking to my back. I walked back through the lower pasture and around the edge of the wooded area behind the cabins till I came to Grandma's pond. The water was still.

I walked down closer.

Esther was sitting in the shade of a large pine tree. She sat on the ground at the base of the tree with her arms wrapped around her knees, staring straight ahead. She didn't look at me as I walked up.

I sat down a few feet from her. She looked like she'd been crying.

"Why did you do it?" I asked. "Why did you help him?"

She glared at me. "I didn't do it for him. Don't you know nothing?"

I didn't know what to say. I still wasn't quite sure I understood. I picked up a small stick and moved aside some pine straw on the ground.

I looked toward the pond. There was a small ripple in the middle. The bream were moving. "Elizabeth says she's going to help you save up what you need for school," I said.

"Oh, really?" she said tartly. "Sure. She lives on pennies. It took me three years of scrimping to save that money, and there ain't no way I can earn all that back. Not around here. I might as well go on."

"Go on where?" I asked. I felt a fluttering in my stomach.

"New York," she said. "Maybe just to Birmingham or Mobile first. Some place where I can get a real job and save enough for a bus ticket."

"You mean you'd go by yourself?"

She gave a cynical laugh. "Who would go with me?"

Going to Mobile didn't sound exciting. Or Birmingham. But going to New York—a city like that one in *Blackboard Jungle*—that sounded as exciting to me as Alaska or Hawaii. I wanted to say, "Me. I'll go with you," but even I wasn't dumb enough to think that could happen.

"But . . . what will Elizabeth say?" I said.

"Who cares? She sure don't care about me." She pushed herself to her feet and brushed the back of her dress. "As far as I'm concerned, the sooner I'm out of here, the better."

She turned and walked quickly back toward her house.

I watched her walk away and wondered if I'd ever see her again. The fluttering was growing, swelling up inside, and I thought I was going to throw up.

Twenty-Four

Esther came to work the next day and the days following, but I expected her to leave at any time. I was always a bit relieved when she walked in at eleven o'clock each morning.

She rarely stayed to eat on the porch with Bennett and me, though, and she never said anything in the kitchen while working unless it was absolutely necessary.

I had an uneasy feeling something was going to explode. At first I thought Esther's leaving would be the cause of it, but as the days lulled by, I wasn't sure. I only knew something terrible was going to happen.

Mama phoned one Friday night in late July to tell me she'd taken a job at a five-and-dime, which meant she and Tony wouldn't be able to come up like she'd planned. She didn't know when she'd get a few days off. She started crying and asked me to pray for Daddy. I asked what was wrong and she said she was just tired, that was all.

After I hung up, Grandma told me Mama had a lot of decisions to make. Of course, I understood a lot more than Mama thought I did. I just didn't like to think about it, much less talk about it.

On the first weekend of August, Winston disappeared. He took all of his clothes. Elizabeth said he'd gone to Birmingham or Montgomery to look for work and that he'd write when he got a job. Bennett told me Esther said Winston couldn't write.

Grandma told me when we were by ourselves that Elizabeth didn't have any idea where Winston was, and she was worried sick about him.

Then the event that got everything started occurred, the event that knocked the breath out of all of us. It wasn't a big event. In fact, at the time no one understood its significance.

It was a phone call on the second Wednesday morning in August from Mrs. Marigold Eastwood. Mrs. Eastwood lived down the road just beyond the store. She and Grandma were both members of the Obadiah Methodist Church. Several times, I had carried to her house groceries that she'd ordered.

I was eating breakfast and heard Grandma say into the telephone mouthpiece, "I'll talk to him, Marigold. I'm sure he'll be glad to."

When she returned to the table, Grandma said, "Mrs. Eastwood wants you to work for her on Saturday. She wants a shed behind her house cleaned out and the rubbish burned. I'm sure she'll pay you more than I do. If you want to help her, it's okay with me."

I agreed.

At lunch that day, I mentioned it to Bennett.

He had his head down over his plate. His fork was halfway to his mouth, loaded with snap beans. His hand froze. He slowly raised his face to look at me.

Then he laid his fork down on the table, pushed back his chair, and left. He didn't go back through the store. He went around the side of the building.

It took me a few moments to realize that he wasn't coming back.

We were busy in the afternoon, and I didn't get a chance to tell Grandma about Bennett's reaction when I had told him about working for Mrs. Eastwood. On the way home, I did. She put her hand on my elbow as we walked along.

"On the Saturday Staple left," Grandma said, "he'd gone to do some work at Marigold's house. She paid him, of course, after he finished. Then he just went away. Lots of men desert their families like that, going up to Detroit or Chicago or Washington, but Staple wasn't that kind of man. I mean, he was a deacon at their church. He was a wonderful husband and father. Just the day before, he'd told your granddaddy how he was planning to save enough money for Esther to go on to high school and then one day to college. He's the one who got her thinking like that. He used to talk about buying his own farm one day with Bennett." She clucked her tongue. "No, sir. I can't imagine what made him run off."

She went through the front gate ahead of me and walked toward the house. "Elizabeth has grieved and grieved over his running off," she continued. "Naturally, it's been a great embarrassment—no, a shame, really— for them. That's why Bennett reacted like that."

We went into the house. Grandma poured us each a glass of lemonade. As she put the pitcher back into the icebox, she glanced out the window over the sink.

"Well, I'll be . . . ," she said. "George, Esther is pacing up and down in front of the barn. I guess she's waiting to see you."

Twenty-Five

As I walked toward the barn, it occurred to me that Esther and I hadn't talked in almost two weeks, not since that afternoon under the tree at the pond when she'd hinted very strongly that she was leaving. I'd seen her each day at the store during the noon hour helping her mother in the kitchen, but she spoke to none of us, not even to Grandma.

Her arms were crossed, and she stopped her pacing as I approached but did not turn toward me or look at me. I stopped a few feet away. I wondered if she'd come to say good-bye. I waited for her to speak.

Finally, she looked at me. "Bennett says you're going to work for Mrs. Eastwood," she said.

"That's right," I said.

She nodded and looked away as if thinking. In a moment, she said, "Did you know that Daddy worked for her the morning before he went away?"

"That's what Grandma told me."

She walked over to the old pin oak on the left side of the barn and sat down Indian-style in front of it.

I sat down beside her.

"My daddy was not the kind of man just to leave his family for no good reason," she said. "He loved us." She paused and bit her lip. She closed her eyes, shook her head slowly for a moment, and swallowed. She opened her eyes and continued. "Whatever he did, he did it because he had to. Probably he did it for us. I know this doesn't sound like it's making any sense, but believe me, my daddy did not just run off and leave his family without some really good reason."

"I'm sure that's true," I said. Of course, I didn't know whether it was true or not.

"He kissed me good-bye when he left for work that morning. Just like he always did. He was smiling. I remember that. He didn't act like some man getting ready to leave. He didn't even take his Bible. He wouldn't have gone anywhere without his Bible."

I looked up toward the house. Grandma had come out onto the back porch with her lemonade and sat down in a rocker.

"Listen to me, George," Esther said. "Something must have happened that morning. I don't know what. But something must have happened while he was at Mrs. Eastwood's working."

"Like what?"

"I don't know. Maybe one of his friends came and told him something. Maybe it was some news about his brother. He's got a brother in Detroit, you know."

"Did y'all write this brother?"

She shook her head. "We haven't heard from him in

years, not since I was a baby, Mama says. We don't know where he is. But what I'm saying is, something must have happened that caused him to leave like that."

She picked up a leaf from the ground and began pulling it apart, slowly, tiny piece by tiny piece. "Mama went to see Mrs. Eastwood afterwards. All she said was that Daddy raked all the leaves in the front yard like she'd asked him to and burned them at the street. Then she paid him and he left. And no, she said, none of his friends came by to see him. She said she didn't remember anything unusual."

Esther turned her face to look at me. Her eyes looked into my eyes. "George, I want you to do this for me," she said. The way she said it was not at all the way Esther the Queen had commanded me and Bennett ever since we were too little to even know what a queen was. The way she said it was like one friend speaking to another. "When you're there I want you to talk to her about my daddy. There might be something she wouldn't tell Mama that she would tell you."

"Like what?" I asked, already feeling very uncomfortable with the idea.

"Maybe she'll tell another white person about something she wouldn't tell Mama. I don't know. Maybe she'll remember something Daddy might've said."

"But that was four years ago. Maybe she won't remember anything about it."

She gave a slight sigh and looked toward Grandma. "That's what Bennett said. He said she probably wouldn't even remember who Staple Garrison was." She looked back at me. "But I want you to ask her anyways. All right?"

I nodded. "Okay," I said softly.

Twenty-Six

I arrived at Mrs. Eastwood's house Saturday morning at eight o'clock. The sun was high and hot already. Mrs. Eastwood was standing in her front yard with a hose, watering a flower bed crowded with zinnias, four-o'clocks, and sweet williams. She was wearing a denim bonnet and brown gardening gloves.

"Good morning, George," she said cheerily. "I hope you've come to work because I have a lot that has to get done today."

She turned off the water and led me around the side of the house.

In back, she showed me an old unpainted board-and-batten shed near the clothesline. "Nobody has even been in there since Mr. Eastwood passed, and that's been twelve years ago," she said. "I opened the door the other day, took one look, saw it was nothing but junk. Nothing but junk. Why Mr. Eastwood saved all those old magazines and newspapers I have no earthly idea. I want it all cleaned out and burned. Everything in there. Cleaned out and burned."

She also showed me a fire pit just beyond the barn

and a gallon jug of gasoline and a wheelbarrow inside the barn.

In the shed was the dry, musty smell of decay. Rat and pigeon turds covered everything. There were several kinds of magazines—*Saturday Evening Post, National Geographic, Progressive Farmer*—yellowed newspapers, boxes of receipts and paid bills going back to the 1920s, packets of letters with old-fashioned handwriting bound up with faded ribbon, empty gallon paint cans, and rope and wire. In the back corners were rat nests. I didn't see any rats, but I knew they were there somewhere.

I got to work. I gathered up the stuff and loaded the wheelbarrow and rolled it to the fire pit, dumped it, and returned to the shed for another load. Within minutes sweat was pouring off me from head to foot and stinging my eyes. Every third load I went to the water tap at the back of the house and got a drink. And over and over as I worked, I rehearsed the words I would say to Mrs. Eastwood when I did what Esther wanted me to do.

About ten o'clock, Mrs. Eastwood brought me a glass of iced tea.

I worked on steadily until she came back to tell me it was noon and she'd made peanut butter and jelly sandwiches for us. She handed me a bar of soap and a hand towel to wash up with at the tap.

I figured I should be finished up in an hour. The fire was already going, burning continually, and the smoke was drifting to the south.

We sat at a white wicker table in wicker chairs on the screened side porch. Mrs. Eastwood had cut the crusts off the sandwiches.

She asked how I was enjoying the summer.

Fine, I told her, and that I liked working at the store with Grandma and with Elizabeth Garrison whose husband had gone to Detroit or some place four years ago.

There was a blankness in her eyes as if she didn't know who I was talking about.

So I blurted, "Grandma says he did some work for you."

"Oh?" She squinted her eyes as she looked at me. "I've had so many.... It's really hard to keep them all straight." She gave a little laugh and covered her mouth as she did.

I took another bite of my sandwich and chewed and swallowed hurriedly. "His name was Staple," I said.

She brightened with recognition and smiled. "Why, yes. Now I remember. I hadn't used him before, but I knew he worked for Tilly and Robert so I got him to rake my leaves. That must have been in November." She patted her mouth with her napkin. "Yes, November. That was that cold winter, wasn't it? Lots of snow? Does it ever snow in Mobile?"

"No'm," I said quickly. "Did Staple say anything that morning? I mean, about having to leave or anything like that?"

Her smile faded and she looked at me curiously. "What?"

I gave a shrug as if it really wasn't important. "I was just wondering," I said. "Since he ran off. It just seems so strange. Grandma said it really upset Granddaddy."

She nodded her head. "Your granddaddy Robert was a good man."

"About Staple," I pressed. "Did any of his friends come to see him that morning?"

"Friends? I hardly think so. I do not permit any socializing when I'm paying people to do work. No, he just raked the leaves and burned them at the street. That's all."

I had finished my sandwich. I could have used another one, but she'd only made one apiece for us. I sipped the milk.

Mrs. Eastwood frowned. "It's funny, now that you ask," she said. "But it seems I do recall someone stopping to talk with him that day."

"Oh?" I asked.

She nodded. "Yes, I remember glancing out the window once—you know how you have to keep checking up on people who're working for you—and he was standing out at the street talking to what's-his-name. He was in his pickup, sitting inside, and Staple was talking with him. Then what's-his-name backed around in my driveway and almost hit the mailbox and ran all over the yard as he drove off."

"Who was it?" I asked.

"You know him. He lives just down the road a

piece." She nodded in the direction of Grandma's. "Right beyond Tilly. Vorhise. Yes. That's it. Turnage Vorhise. He takes care of your grandmother's cows, doesn't he?"

Twenty-Seven

It was almost three o'clock before I finished. Mrs. Eastwood paid me two dollars.

I stopped by the store on the way home to get a Coke. Grandma told me to take the bottle with me and go get cleaned up, that I smelled like smoke and was stinking up the store. I bathed quickly. I wanted to go down to Elizabeth's and tell Esther what Mrs. Eastwood had said.

I stepped out the back door and gave a start. Both Esther and Bennett were sitting on the far side of the porch on the floor with their legs dangling off the side. Both were looking at me expectantly.

I walked over and sat down beside Esther.

"Well?" she asked.

I told them what Mrs. Eastwood said about Mr. Vorhise stopping by to talk with their father.

Neither said anything for a long time. Then Bennett said, "That man never say nothing to me about knowing Daddy. Never."

"Hush," Esther said. "I'm thinking." She was staring toward the barn.

After what seemed like a very long time, she said, "Why would Mr. Vorhise stop and talk to Daddy?"

Bennett grunted and said, "Ain't but one reason and one reason only—to tell him do something."

Esther jumped off the porch. "Come on," she said. "I want to see something."

We hurried to keep up with her. Her stride was much longer than ours. We went up the drive and onto the road and down toward Mr. Vorhise's house.

Tall sprawling privet bushes grew up through a crumbling picket fence along the front. We paused momentarily at the driveway. It was a dogtrot house and reaching out over the front porch were the massive limbs of three large trees.

"I don't like this," I said. "What if he sees us?"

Esther turned on her heel and led us back toward Grandma's. "What was it Daddy was doing when the man stopped?" she asked.

"Raking leaves," Bennett said, walking beside her, trying to keep up.

"Exactly," she said. "Those are oak trees back there."

"Is that what he done?" asked Bennett. "He asked him to come rake leaves for him?"

Esther didn't answer. She kept walking.

"You're thinking it was Mr. Vorhise who was the last person to talk to Daddy before he left," said Bennett. "Ain't that right?"

Still, she didn't answer.

When we were in the backyard again, Esther placed

her hands on her hips and started pacing back and forth. "Okay," she said. "This may be right. Daddy was raking leaves, and Mr. Vorhise comes driving by and thinks he needs to hire him to rake his own yard. So he stops and tells him to come on to his house when he gets through at Mrs. Eastwood's."

We both nodded. That seemed to make sense. Staple would have had to rake Mr. Vorhise's yard just because Mr. Vorhise told him to. After all, Mr. Vorhise was white and Staple was colored.

"So," she said, "how are we going to find out for sure that Daddy went there to work?"

"We for sure ain't asking Mr. Vorhise," said Bennett. He looked at me. "Could you talk to him?"

I drew a sharp breath. Talking to Mrs. Eastwood was one thing. Talking to Mr. Vorhise was something else entirely different.

"No, no," said Esther, and I breathed a sigh of relief.

"But there is someone who might tell us." She gave each of us a knowing nod. "He might just do that for me."

"Who are you talking about?" asked Bennett.

"My handsome man," she said. There was a cold look in her eyes.

"What? You planning to go back there? After all we been through?"

"We have to," she said.

"He's an idiot," Bennett said. "How can he tell you anything?"

"Who's going with me?"

"Not me," said Bennett. "Never."

"George?" she asked, looking at me. It was a look of immense sadness.

I tried to speak, but I wasn't breathing right. I managed a faint nod of my head.

Twenty-Eight

Esther returned to her house. We waited while she went inside. In a moment, she came out with a paper sack in her hand.

"What's in the sack?" asked Bennett.

"I'll show you when we get there," she said, turning up the road.

"Humph," he said, walking behind her. "I told you I ain't going."

"Then you won't know, will you?"

Bennett was true to his word. He went with us as far as the barbed-wire fence, but no farther. "I'm telling you, George, them crazy dogs gonna eat y'all up. You need be staying right here on our land."

I didn't answer him. Instead, I moved on after Esther through the woods.

I had no idea how she planned to contact Jimmy or, if she did, how he would react. After all, the last time we were at the pond he became terrified and ran off to get his father. Would just the sight of us frighten him this time?

One thing I definitely knew was that if he did run off, I was tearing back through the woods as fast as possible.

We reached the mouth of the stream. All was quiet at the pond. The sun glared white hot on the face of the water. The reeds sprouting high in spots around the bank were motionless. Not a breath of air moved. The hum of insects grew loud as we stopped walking.

Esther stepped out onto the bank, and I followed. She looked up the hillside and started to climb. I climbed after her. I wondered what I would say to Grandma if Mr. Vorhise caught me on his property again. I decided I would tell her we were trying to find out something about Staple. I hoped that the truth would do.

The grass was waist high and coarse and pulled at my pants and arms.

As we neared the crest of the hill, Esther bent down, and I did, too. Only our heads were visible above the grass. The sun was scorching, and sweat rolled down my face and into my eyes

We could see the house, but no people, no movement.

I'm not sure how long we watched. It seemed like five hours. It may have only been an hour. Finally, Esther said, "Let's go." I led the way down the hill to the pond.

We went back to the mouth of the stream and drank

several handfuls of the cool water flowing into the pond, then sat in the shade of a big sycamore.

"What's in the bag?" I asked.

She opened the sack and pulled out, one by one, three framed photographs of men, then laid them in the grass in front of us. I recognized the photographs. They were from the mantle in Esther's house. I recognized Staple in one of the pictures.

Esther put her hand on the photograph of a man with a high, stiff white collar. "This is Mama's father," she said. "He died before I was born. And this other one is his father." She pointed to the photo of an elderly man with a white beard.

We continued to wait. Jimmy never came.

Finally, Esther said, "Come on. We'll come back later."

Bennett was waiting for us when we got back. "I been just listening to hear that shotgun," he said.

The next afternoon was Sunday. At three o'clock I went back with Esther to Mr. Vorhise's pond. Again we climbed the hill and waited and watched. Nothing.

Again we sat under the sycamore. Esther talked of going to San Francisco one day and—this was the first time I'd ever heard her say this—of becoming a school teacher. She also told me to forget all that foolishness about joining the merchant marines and that I needed to start thinking about going to college.

She had different pictures this time. She said her

mother might notice if she kept borrowing the pictures on the mantle.

We returned to the pond on Monday after work. We didn't stay on the hill but a little while. Clothes hung on the clothesline beside the Vorhise house. Otherwise, everything looked the same.

We sat under the sycamore. Esther was talking about how she remembered riding on her father's shoulders when she was small and—

She stopped talking. She was looking up at the hillside. I looked, too.

A head was sticking up out of the grass looking at us. It was Jimmy.

Esther waved. Jimmy waved.

She stood up slowly and stepped farther along the bank. I followed. She motioned for Jimmy to come.

At first, he just sat there. Then he stood up and began walking toward us. He walked hesitantly as if ready to bolt.

"Aren't you still my handsome man?" Esther asked.

He began to smile.

"Come here," she said, motioning for him to come to her. "I want you to look at something."

He walked up to her, a bashful grin on his face.

She took the photo of her grandfather out of the bag and held it up for him to see.

He looked at it, then looked questioningly at her.

She took out the second photo.

He looked at it also. No reaction.

She showed him the photo of Staple.

His eyes grew big, and he recoiled. "Bad man! Bad man!" he shouted at Esther. "Bad man!"

Esther shoved the picture back into the bag. "It's okay, Jimmy," she said in a calm voice. "It's okay. I've put the picture away."

The boy's eyes looked from Esther to me and back to Esther. I thought he was ready to run.

"Listen to me," Esther said, smiling at him. "Where are my flowers, Jimmy? Can you pick me some flowers?"

He cocked his head as he looked at her. Slowly a smile came to his lips.

He turned and went up the hillside and was gone.

"Let's go," I said. I knew we'd been lucky so far.

"Wait," she said.

So we waited.

In a few minutes, Jimmy returned with a handful of weed flowers. Esther took the flowers and thanked him.

We left.

I glanced back over my shoulder once as we were moving into the woods. He was standing at the mouth of the stream watching us go.

Esther walked fast back to her house. I hurried after her.

"What does this mean?" I asked. "That he'd seen Staple before?"

She shook her head but didn't answer.

She didn't have to. I already knew the answer.

We reached the house. Bennett was waiting for us on the porch. Esther told him what had happened.

He looked at me, waiting for an explanation. I shrugged my shoulders as if I didn't know.

Finally, Esther said, "I know Daddy went there that day. And I don't have any doubts that Jimmy recognized him from the picture. I don't know why he remembers him as bad."

"You can't always recognize people that clear from photographs," said Bennett. "Maybe he—"

"We need to go back," she interrupted.

"Go back where?" Bennett asked.

"To Mr. Vorhise's land."

"Why?" I asked, feeling a tightness in my chest.

"Daddy may have been there just before he left. I want to go over it all. Even that pine grove. Especially the pine grove. Somehow . . ." She didn't finish.

Bennett looked at me. "Can you explain to this dumb Midnight Face that there ain't nothing there but an old dump?" he said. "That's all, just somebody's old, rotten garbage."

"Why is Jimmy so terrified of that place?" she asked.

"Maybe he don't like garbage? Maybe he's afraid of tin cups?" he said with a derisive snort. "That's all that was there."

"Tin cups?" I asked. "What cups?"

"That's what I dug up," he said. "One cup with the handle rusted off."

"I thought it was a tin can," I said.

"No," said Esther. "It was a cup. Actually, it was a dipper. Only the handle was, like Bennett said, rusted off."

"A . . . dipper . . . ?" I asked.

At that moment if one of them had hit me in the forehead with a brick I couldn't have been more stunned.

Twenty-Nine

I couldn't sleep that night. I lay in the darkness listening to the sounds floating in through the open windows—the sounds of dogs far off, of an occasional car going by, of crickets and owls.

I hadn't told Esther and Bennett what Daddy said just before the boat capsized. Why not? Well, for one thing, that's not the kind of thing you can jump out there and tell your friends. I mean, I didn't know for sure the man drinking out of the white man's well was Staple.

I wondered about phoning long distance and asking Daddy if the man who told him that story was Mr. Vorhise. Did Daddy even know Mr. Vorhise?

Yes. Of course. Grandma said Mr. Vorhise had been in school with Mama. And Mama and Daddy were in school together. Daddy was just one year older. The high school at Obadiah wasn't very big. They had to know each other.

That thought upset me all the more.

I went to bed early, and Grandma asked me what was wrong. I just told her I didn't feel good.

And I worried that somehow Jimmy would be able to tell his father that Esther and I had been back to his pond. All through the night I expected at any moment to hear a knock on the front door—Mr. Vorhise coming back to see Grandma about me.

I went in and out of sleep. I heard the clock in the hallway strike twelve times, then once, then twice, and I kept reminding myself again and again that when Bennett dug in the pine grove, he hadn't uncovered a body. Only a tin dipper. And every old farmhouse had a dipper. Whatever cabin had dumped garbage near that pond certainly would have had a dipper. That's all it was.

I thought I heard something outside. Cat? Possum?

I sat up in bed and stared out the window. I could see the barn clearly in the moonlight. All was still, and—

Was that something beside the barn door? Yes! It moved. A shadow, almost.

I got out of bed, moved to the window, and put my face right against the screen. I peered at the place where I thought I'd seen something. In a moment, it moved again. Yes. A person, and quickly whoever it was disappeared around the side of the barn.

I knew it was Auntie Hoosilla. Had to be. What on earth was she doing out at night like this? And why was she in our backyard?

I thought about waking Grandma but didn't. Auntie Hoosilla's behavior never seemed to upset her. I got back into bed.

I may have fallen off to sleep some. I'm not sure.

At breakfast Grandma looked at me and said maybe she ought to take me to see Dr. Tatum. I said I was all right.

"I thought I saw Auntie Drusilla out by the barn late last night," I said.

She sipped her orange juice and had a pleased look on her face. "Yes," she said, putting down the glass. "She's never too far away."

"Doesn't that bother you?"

"I rather like it," she said.

I ate my toast and wanted to ask her about Mr. Vorhise but wasn't sure how to do it without telling her I had been back to his pond.

Then I remembered the day Mr. Vorhise had that dog at the store.

"I wonder how Dog is doing," I said, quite pleased that I had found such a nice opening.

"I'm sure he's fine," she said. "I think he has somebody who is loving him and who really needs a dog. Needs him, no doubt, much more than you or I do."

"He sure was scared of Mr. Vorhise's fighting dog."

She didn't say anything.

I continued. "Bennett says Mr. Vorhise has four fighting dogs. Has he always raised fighting dogs?"

"The Vorhises have always been a bit different," she said, buttering a piece of toast. "I want you to try these watermelon-rind preserves. I just opened them." She pushed the canning jar closer to me.

"You said he was in school with Mama. That means he was in school with Daddy, too. Were they friends?"

There. I had finally gotten it out. I held my breath now, waiting for her answer.

She took a small bite of her toast and chewed slowly, swallowed, and said, "I'm not sure you would call them friends. Not like Kruncher Burns and your father are friends. But, yes. They were together some. I think your father goes deer hunting with him when he comes up with y'all at Christmas."

She began buttering another piece of toast. "Here, let me fix you one of these with the preserves. Tell me what you think. I put them up myself."

The fact that my father may have known Mr. Vorhise in high school was one thing. The fact that he may have gone hunting with him last Christmas was something else entirely. That fact was like a stack of firewood setting right on top of my chest all morning as I did my work at the store. My breathing was shallow. The only hope I clung to was that what was buried in the pine grove was nothing more than a bunch of old bottles, tin cans, and maybe an old wagon-wheel hub or something.

At lunch Esther stayed to eat, but she only picked at her food.

"This is something we have to do," she said, her eyes on her brother. "You know that."

"I ain't going back on Mr. Vorhise's land," he said.

"Daddy loved you," she said. Now there was a certain tenderness in her eyes.

He took a forkful of sweet potatoes, half swallowed, and said, "Maybe he didn't even go there. You ever think about that? Maybe Mr. Vorhise told him to come rake leaves the next week or something. You ever think of that?"

Esther didn't answer right away. "I just have this feeling," she said, looking away. "And why was Jimmy so afraid of that pine grove?"

"Maybe he got stung by a wasp there or something." Bennett elbowed me. "George, tell her she ain't thinking right."

I laid my fork down and wet my lips with my tongue. I had cotton mouth bad. "About that dipper . . . ," I said slowly. I cleared my throat. "I . . . I heard a man say once that a colored man got killed for drinking out of somebody's dipper."

Both of them stared at me, trying to comprehend exactly what I was saying.

Esther leaned forward, her face coming close to mine. "What man? What man said this?"

I could feel my face reddening. I shrugged. "Just a man." I cleared my throat again. I couldn't say it was my father. I just couldn't do it.

Thirty

Bennett agreed to go back on one condition. He would go only on a night when he was positive Mr. Vorhise and his dogs would be gone. And, he said, the only time both the man and the dogs were gone from the farm was when there was a dog fight. He would go on dog-fight night.

That made sense to me. Esther didn't seem bothered by dogs at all, but she did seem pleased that her brother had agreed to go. I knew, of course, she would go with or without him, or with or without me.

Wednesday morning, Bennett told us that he had been riding in the back of Mr. Vorhise's pickup earlier that morning when Mr. Vorhise stopped in town for gas.

Another man was at the filling station, and he said something to Mr. Vorhise about betting.

"He said this," Bennett recalled. "'Turnage, I sure hope that mongrel of yours can give my big yellow a decent fight. He's about to get flabby from lack of competition.' And Mr. Vorhise said, 'Are you willing to put up another twenty-five dollars?' The man said, 'I'll match that and add another twenty-five.' And Mr.

Vorhise said, 'Well, come Saturday night, we'll see whose dog is there to fight.'"

Esther and I sat there listening to him, looking at him.

After a few moments, she said, "Okay. It's this Saturday night. George, we need your grandmother's flashlight again."

Over the next three days I thought of nothing else but what we were going to do Saturday night. I'm sure that was the main thing on the minds of Esther and Bennett also, but we didn't talk about it. We talked about other things. I rambled on about motorcycles, describing the one Daddy used to have and the one I was going to buy.

Esther told us stories of a batty old woman she cleaned house for two afternoons a week on the other side of town. The woman, she said, was over eighty and had seven cats, all black except one white one.

Bennett hardly said a word.

Saturday was unbearable as I went about my duties at work. It was overcast, muggy, and hot, and the stack of firewood on my chest seemed to grow by the hour.

At supper that evening, I forced myself to chatter away with Grandma about my motorcycle and how I was going to be riding it to school. Grandma wasn't very happy about my buying a motorcycle. "You need to be saving your money for college," she said.

I told her Bennett and Esther and me might play kick-the-can later. That wasn't a complete lie. I didn't say we were going to, only that we might. She said to be careful.

She was sitting in the front room reading her Sunday school quarterly when I left. I took the flashlight.

Esther and Bennett were waiting for me on their porch. Bennett had taken the shovel up to the barbed-wire fence that afternoon while his mother was away. He didn't want to have to explain to her why we were taking it with us if she saw us walking away from the house.

As it turned out, she was sitting on the front porch when we left and asked where we were going. "We might spot some deer," Bennett said.

It was still only dusk when we reached the path leading to the fence and the woods beyond, but, with the dark low clouds, night was falling rapidly.

We moved quickly through the woods. Each of us knew the way very well after so many trips back and forth.

At the pond, Bennett said he wanted to go up to the top of the hill and look across the field to be sure Mr. Vorhise had already left. Esther and I stood on the bank and waited while he went to the top of the hill.

He came running down. "He ain't gone yet," he said. There was a desperation in his voice, almost a panic. "His pickup is still parked at the back of the house."

"You can see that?"

"The light over the back door is on," he said.

"When is he leaving?" she asked.

"I don't know. He's got the kennels on the truck."

There was a rumble of thunder in the distance.

The three of us went back up the hill and knelt in the grass looking toward the house. In the bed of the pickup, clearly visible in the yellowish light, were the wooden kennels for the dogs.

"Look," said Bennett, "The dogs are still in the runs. He ain't loaded them up yet."

Another light hung near the dog runs. I could make out the dogs, one in each run, moving back and forth, and none of them was Dog. I really didn't expect him to be there.

There was a flash of lightning followed by thunder. Much closer.

"What's God saying?" said Bennett without a trace of skepticism, only hope.

Esther waited a moment to answer, then said, "He says tonight is the night. Regardless."

"What do you mean, 'regardless'?" he asked.

She didn't answer. Suddenly the wind picked up, and the grasses around us danced.

"Where do they have these fights?" I asked.

"I guess in somebody's barn," Bennett said.

The wind became stronger, and the air was thick and moist with the smell of rain. At any moment the storm would be upon us.

"It ain't going to be easy digging in the mud," Bennett said.

"Then let's get started," Esther said.

"What about the dogs . . . ?"

"George, stay here and watch," she said. "If he does come out of the house and start moving this way, you whistle."

"We can't hear a whistle," said Bennett. "George, you come get us."

"Okay," I said. I could feel the blood pounding in my temples.

I handed Esther the flashlight, and they went down the hill and made their way over the dam to the pine grove. I felt a drop of rain hit the back of my neck.

Lightning flashed, lighting up the Vorhise farmhouse, outbuildings, barn, and dog runs as if it were daylight, and the crash of thunder shook the ground I was kneeling on. The dogs were in their houses now, not out in the runs.

Down behind me I could see light from the flashlight moving in and behind the pine trees. Then it was steady, still, and I knew Esther would be holding it while Bennett handled the shovel.

The wind shifted and was now blowing from the pond toward the house. One of the dogs came out of its doghouse and started barking.

The others came out. All four of them were barking loud.

Oh, God, I prayed. We need more lightning, a roll of thunder, to drive those dogs back inside!

There was more lightning, and the dogs ran inside

but came out again and barked. It was a furious barking, a continuous barking.

I looked back toward the pines and the light. I wondered what Esther and Bennett were finding. Garbage, I hoped. Lots and lots of garbage. "Hurry," I whispered out loud even though they couldn't hear me. "Hurry now."

I looked again to the house. The back door opened, and Mr. Vorhise walked out to the runs. He was talking to the dogs, trying to calm them down. I couldn't make out his words.

It was beginning to rain now. Big heavy drops. And the wind gusted and the rain stung as it hit my face.

Mr. Vorhise was looking in our direction.

I looked toward the darkness where Bennett and Esther were and could see the light through the rain. I wanted them to be through, for the light to start moving out of the pines, so we could get on home.

Mr. Vorhise went back into the house.

I jerked my head back to the pines. I thought I heard something.

Wind. Yes, but . . . there it was again. A wail.

I looked back toward the house. Mr. Vorhise was coming out again, and he had a flashlight in one hand and a gun in the other. The dogs were going crazy.

I scrambled down the hillside. Toward the bottom my feet slipped out from under me and I thudded to the ground.

I got to my feet and ran over the dam toward the pines.

"Get up!" Bennett was screaming at Esther. "Get up!"

She was kneeling on the ground. Bennett held the flashlight with one hand and was pulling at her arm with the other.

"Mr. Vorhise is coming!" I said.

Then, in the light of Bennett's flashlight, I could see, in front of Esther on the ground, pieces of a rotted blanket and bones. Some kind of bones.

Esther wailed louder, rocking back and forth.

"Help me!" Bennett said to me. "Get her up!"

I grabbed her under the armpits and pulled her back. "We have to go!" I said to her. "Stand up!"

Bennett held the flashlight in one hand and, with short, quick strokes, was raking dirt and mud over the bones. The wind and rain were vicious now, whipping and pounding.

Esther got to her feet and stood there, not moving.

With the back of the shovel blade, Bennett patted down the mud and leaves covering the bones. I helped him drag the small dead oak tree back over the spot.

"Bring Esther," he said, clicking off the light.

Bennett plunged into the total darkness of the woods, and I grabbed Esther's wrist and pulled her after me.

Thirty-One

I have no idea how many times Esther fell and dragged me down with her. Each time I pushed myself up and pulled her up again.

We ran on and fell, got up and ran.

I couldn't hear anything but the wind and the rain.

I helped Esther through the barbed-wire fence, and then we walked through the tall grass to the road. Rainwater was coursing down the ruts in the road as it descended toward the cabins.

Bennett clicked on the flashlight, and we walked in single file, Bennett leading and Esther in the middle and me behind. We walked along the edge on the grass, trying to avoid the deep puddles in the road and the slick mud. Bennett led us to the barn and the toolroom in the rear. There was an overhead light in the toolroom.

We sat down against the rear wall. The single light bulb suspended on a cord from the ceiling cast the room in a soft red-orange glow. The room smelled of harnesses and oil.

Bennett bumped the back of his head against the wall several times. He groaned but didn't say anything.

Esther sat cross-legged with her hands in her lap. Her left hand was still balled up in a fist. She was staring straight ahead.

All of us were sopping wet and caked with mud.

I cleared my throat. "It might not have been him, you know. I mean, Staple. People have been living around here forever. That could have been an Indian even. Didn't that look like an Indian blanket?"

Bennett drew a deep breath and let it out. "That's right. I think there was even slaves buried all around here. Them bones could be over a hundred years old."

"Maybe a Civil War soldier," I suggested.

Bennett sighed again. "Do you reckon Mr. Vorhise went down to where we were? Do you think he found where we were digging?"

"I doubt it," I said. "We were gone before he got there. You cut off the light. Maybe he just came to the edge of the hillside and shined his light down around the pond. As hard as it was raining, I don't think he'd have wanted to get down in all that mud."

"What about the dogs?" asked Bennett. "They didn't sound like they was coming."

"I didn't see him take any out of the runs. I doubt he'd want to let them run loose just before taking them off to fight. You know, he might get one running a rabbit or a deer and not get him back."

"Yeah," said Bennett, taking another deep breath. "And I don't see how that all was supposed to be Daddy." He looked at Esther. "I think you're right, girl. Someday you're going to be walking down a street in Detroit City and there is going to be Daddy as big as life. Yessiree. And he's going to come back home and—"

She raised her left fist and held it out in front of her. She was looking straight ahead.

She turned her fist over and slowly opened her fingers until they were fully extended.

Bennett and I stared at her palm, and I felt as if someone had his viselike fingers around my neck and was choking me. I couldn't breathe.

Centered on her upturned palm was a grimy and mud-smeared silver dog's-head belt buckle. I had seen it many times—attached to the belt Staple Garrison had worn every day.

Thirty-Two

Bennett pushed himself to his feet and left the room, moving fast.

Esther began wiping the belt buckle clean with her shirttail and rubbing it with her fingers. "I saw it when Bennett turned over the dirt with the bones in it," she said very softly. "I grabbed it. I knew what it was, and I knew Daddy was dead and had been dead all this time." She was crying.

"We need to go to the police," I said.

She looked at me curiously. "You don't understand, do you?" she asked.

"What?"

She gave a shake of her head and pushed herself up. "Never mind," she said. She sounded very tired.

I followed her out of the barn. "But we've got to tell Grandma," I said.

She clutched the belt buckle against her chest. "I've got to tell Mama first," she said. "Then I want to go with you."

When we got to Elizabeth's, Bennett was sitting on the front steps with his face in his hands.

Esther stopped beside him and put her hand on his shoulder. "Come on with me," she said.

He got up and followed her into the house.

I stood in the rain at the bottom of the steps, looking through the screen door into the small front room with yellowed newspapers tacked to the walls in hopes of keeping out some of the winter's wind. I could see Bennett standing in the middle of the room, and I knew Esther was near him. Together, I knew, they were talking with their mother.

Elizabeth's scream was the most terrible cry of pain I'd ever heard. It jarred me, making my knees weak. Tears came into my eyes then. I could hear not only Elizabeth crying with loud, moaning sobs, but I could hear Esther and Bennett, too, crying with their mother. Elizabeth wailed out Staple's name and also Winston's.

I stepped forward and put both hands on the edge of the porch and began to quake from head to foot. It was as if a tight net of razor-sharp hurting was enclosing me, squeezing me in.

I needed to tell Grandma. She'd know what to do.

I left and hurried back to the house. Grandma was talking on the telephone.

She looked up at me, then said, "I've got to go," and hung up.

"George . . . ," she said, reaching out to me. "What's wrong? What happened to you? Your clothes . . ."

"We found Staple's body," I blurted. I told her everything. I talked fast. I told her about finding the bones. I told her about Esther finding the belt buckle. I told her about Elizabeth wailing down at her house.

She sat down slowly in one of the chairs at the kitchen table. "That buckle was your grandfather's," she said. "He gave it to Staple."

Then I told her what my father had said, about the man he knew being drunk and killing a man for drinking out of his dipper.

She sat there for a few moments as if the full weight of what had happened was just now falling upon her. The pain seemed to crush her.

She stood up. "I have got to see Elizabeth. Then I'll call the sheriff."

She pulled on her rubber boots at the back door and took her umbrella. I followed.

Grandma started crying before we got to Elizabeth's. She went to the chair where Elizabeth sat and kneeled down on the floor in front of her and put her arms around her. They held each other and cried.

I stood just inside the door with Esther and Bennett.

In a while, Grandma told Elizabeth she had to call the sheriff. We went back home.

Sheriff Hale Boggs was twelve miles away in Farmington, the county seat.

The man who answered the phone at the sheriff's office said both Sheriff Boggs and the other deputy were out on calls and he himself couldn't leave the office, but he'd have Sheriff Boggs phone when he got back.

I took a bath and then sat in the kitchen with Grandma. She made coffee for us while we waited. She turned on the radio, and we listened to the *Grand Ole Opry.*

Just before ten o'clock, the phone rang.

Grandma answered the phone, told the caller who she was, then said, "Listen, these children found a body. It's the body of Staple Garrison. He disappeared four years ago and—"

She paused a moment. "They found it on Turnage Vorhise's place," she continued. "That's right next to me." She paused again. "Staple Garrison. He worked for us." Pause. "Description? He was Negro, late thirties. Why?" Pause. "Yes, four years ago, and they found a belt buckle I know was his. That's how we know."

She gave an exasperated sigh and shook her head. "No, now you listen to me. We need you to come over here—" Another sigh. She listened. Finally, she nodded her head and said, "All right. Then we'll expect you first thing in the morning."

She hung up the phone hard.

"What?" I asked.

"He says he's got live people he's trying to keep from killing each other at all these honky-tonks and that he can't come right now. He said he'll be here first thing in the morning."

She wiped her eyes and said, "Come with me. We need to go get Reverend Mann. Elizabeth needs her preacher."

"What about Mr. Vorhise?" I asked.

"What do you mean?"

"What's he going to do when the sheriff comes?" In my mind the man was as vicious as his dogs. I was primarily thinking of what he would try to do to Esther, Bennett, and me.

I don't think Grandma understood. She didn't answer.

Thirty-Three

Reverend Mann and his wife followed us in their car, an old Buick, back to Grandma's. He left his car at the top of the hill rather than drive down to the row of cabins. Grandma told him as slick as it was, he'd never get back up the hill.

Reverend and Mrs. Mann stayed at the Garrisons' till just after eleven. Grandma and I didn't leave till midnight. Elizabeth told us she would be okay, that she had her big, strong children, that they had each other.

The next day was Sunday. I got up before six o'clock. Grandma was already up, frying bacon. I'm not sure she ever went to bed. "You can help me take some breakfast down to Elizabeth's," she said.

We took the breakfast, ate with them, then returned to the house to wait. We sat in the rockers on the front porch with our eyes fixed on the road, looking in the direction of town, since Sheriff Boggs would come through town from Farmington before he got to our house.

Several women from Elizabeth's church nodded to us as they passed in front of the house and turned down the lane leading to Elizabeth's. They were already dressed for church. They would stay with her till church time.

We expected the sheriff around eight o'clock. He didn't come. He hadn't come by eight-thirty either. Grandma phoned his house in Farmington. His wife told her he was eating breakfast and would be along when he finished.

Esther walked around the side of the house. She was wearing a Sunday dress. She sat down on the top step. She didn't say anything.

Just after nine-thirty, Sheriff Hale Boggs and Deputy W. B. Yerby arrived. They walked up to the porch and both tipped their hats to Grandma. Sheriff Boggs was no taller than me, probably didn't weigh much more, and was smoking a cigarette. Deputy Yerby was tall and heavy.

Grandma, Esther, and I all stood as they approached.

"Tell us what happened," the sheriff said.

"Would you like to go inside?" asked Grandma.

"No, ma'am," he said, looking at me. "Is this one of the kids who was at the pond?"

"Why . . . yes," she said.

That was when I knew something wasn't quite right. Something was bad not right. Grandma had not said anything about a pond to Sheriff Boggs when she talked to him on the phone last night.

"Tell me what happened," he said to Grandma.

She began at the beginning, telling him how we had fished at Vorhise's pond, how we shouldn't have, she knew, but then we found the dipper, and how we went back last night, after hearing Turnage Vorhise had talked to Staple on the day he disappeared, and dug up his bones. They knew it was him because of the belt buckle.

"Where is this belt buckle?" he asked.

Esther opened her hand.

He picked it up, looked at it for a moment, then gave it back to her. "I can't tell you how many of these I've seen around. What about you, W. B.?"

The deputy looked at me with his pale blue eyes. "They're a dime a dozen." His eyes shivered my spine.

"Well," said the sheriff, "I guess we'd better go talk to Vorhise."

I looked at Grandma. A flushed color was rising up from her throat into her face. "We'll go with you," she said.

"I don't think that's necessary." He flipped his cigarette butt into the yard and took another cigarette out of his shirt pocket.

"I think it is," she said. In her eyes was a fury I'd never seen before. I didn't understand what was going on.

Sheriff Boggs shrugged. "Suit yourself," he said. "I suppose every accused person has a right to face his accuser."

He and the deputy started back toward their car.

Grandma looked at Esther. "You go stay with your mother, child," she said. "George and I are going over to Mr. Vorhise's."

Esther drew herself up, making her just as tall as Grandma. "I want to go, too," she said, her eyes locked on Grandma's eyes.

Grandma touched her arm. "I know you do. But you can't. Not this time. Now go stay with your mother. And take good care of that belt buckle."

We drove in the car even though Mr. Vorhise's wasn't far. Grandma didn't want to walk in the mud on the road.

Mr. Vorhise opened the front door, looked at each of us, and asked, "What can I do for you?"

The sheriff smiled pleasantly and explained that me and two colored children had dug up some bones on his place and that he wanted to know if Mr. Vorhise knew anything about it.

Mr. Vorhise looked at Grandma. His eyes narrowed and his brow furrowed. "You promised me those kids wouldn't be trespassing on my property anymore," he said.

Grandma's cheek was taut. "Seems like there was a good reason you didn't want anybody on your place," she said.

"Wait a minute," interrupted the sheriff, giving Grandma a look to let her know to keep quiet. He turned to Mr. Vorhise. "Do you know anything about any bodies buried by your pond?"

"I'm not saying there ain't, and I'm not saying there is," he said. "There was Creek Indians all through here, you know. You can find arrowheads and pieces of pots and anything in this ground. Bones, too. All kind of bones. Dog bones, cow bones, possum bones."

"What about it, son?" the sheriff said to me, winking at the deputy. "You think you can tell the difference between a possum's bones and those of a man?" Both he and Deputy Yerby laughed.

Grandma's breathing was getting quicker. My face felt like it was on fire.

"What about you talking with this colored boy the day he disappeared?" the sheriff asked Mr. Vorhise, referring to Staple. "What can you tell me about that?"

He shrugged one shoulder. "I may have. I don't rightly remember. I've worked so many of them. You know how it is."

"Well," said the sheriff, "I guess we'd better have a look at this body. You got a shovel we can use?"

"Sure," said Mr. Vorhise. "It's around back."

"Okay, son," the sheriff said to me. "You lead the way."

Thirty-Four

We walked around the side of the house with Mr. Vorhise leading and Grandma, me, and the two lawmen following. When we rounded the corner to the back of the house, I saw a water pump in the middle of the backyard. It had a bucket under it, and a dipper handle was sticking out of the bucket. I wondered if that was the very spot where Mr. Vorhise shot Staple Garrison for drinking water from his dipper.

Mr. Vorhise picked up a shovel that was leaning against the door of a shed and looked at me. There was something of a smile on his lips. "Lead on," he said.

We walked past the dog runs. Dogs in two of the runs barked and jumped at their fences as we passed. Both were terrifying to look at. A third dog was lying half inside the door of his kennel. He barely raised his head to look at us. One of his ears was matted with blood and flies swarmed around his head. There was no dog in the fourth run, but the night before I had seen dogs in each run. I wondered where the dog was.

We walked through the pasture. Grandma didn't seem concerned about her shoes at all. About halfway to the pond, one of her shoes came off, stuck in the mud. She pulled it out and took off her other shoe and walked in her stocking feet.

I paused at the top of the hillside and looked down. The still, smooth surface of the pond reflected the grasses on the bank and the trees behind as distinctly as a mirror. I remembered the storm from last night.

The sheriff tried to take Grandma's arm to help her down the hill, but she shook him off with a gesture that said, "Don't put your hands on me."

I led them over the dam to the pine grove. Everything was wet and muddy. "Under that tree," I said, pointing to the small dead oak on the ground.

Deputy Yerby pulled the tree to one side and took the shovel from Mr. Vorhise.

He placed his foot on the edge of the shovel and pushed it into the ground. He turned over a shovelful of wet dirt. The soil was loose. There was nothing but soil. He turned over another and another. Only dirt. No bones, no rusty dipper, not even a trace of a rotted blanket.

Thirty-Five

Sheriff Boggs raised his eyebrows and looked at me. "You sure this is the place?" he asked. There was almost a twinkle in his eyes.

I didn't understand. I had been here last night. In the light of the flashlight, I'd seen with my own eyes a jumble of bones in the dirt, right at this very spot.

I looked quickly at the ground around the rest of the clearing. Was it someplace else? My mind was reeling.

Grandma took a deep breath, released it, and said to me, "Come on, George." She took one step, then paused, and looked back at Mr. Vorhise. "I believe in the judgment of God," she said through her teeth. "And believe me you are going to feel it." Her voice was shaking. "And stay away from my cows. You're fired."

We walked back to Mr. Vorhise's house. The sheriff and deputy and Mr. Vorhise followed a little ways behind us.

At the front of the house, Grandma opened the back door of her car and threw in one shoe and then the other. Hard.

She turned to Sheriff Boggs. "I would like you to stop by my place before you leave for Farmington, if you don't mind."

He put his hand to the brim of his hat and gave a nod. "Happy to," he said.

"I'm furious," she said to me, as she drove back to the house. "I just want to give him a piece of my mind. I want him to know I'm talking with the editor of the *Pontola County Times.* I want everybody in this whole county to know what he's trying to do."

"But what about the pond?" I asked her. "How did he know about the pond before you told him?"

"Obviously he phoned Mr. Vorhise after I talked to him last night," she said as she parked in the garage. "And Mr. Vorhise had all morning long while the sheriff was enjoying his breakfast to dig up poor Staple." There were tears in her eyes. "No telling what he's done with him."

"What about the belt buckle?" I asked. "And what about Daddy? He said some man told him about killing a colored man, and we found a dipper with the bones. Daddy could tell us whether it was Mr. Vorhise or not."

Esther and Bennett were standing in the backyard waiting for us. They followed us around to the front of the house.

"What do you mean?" exclaimed Esther after I told her.

"They were gone," I said, referring to the bones. "Nothing was there. Not the dipper or blanket. Nothing."

Bennett's mouth was open, and he looked at me as if I were lying.

The sheriff's car stopped in front of the house, and the two lawmen got out.

"You phoned him last night, didn't you?" Grandma said to the sheriff. "You told him we were coming this morning, didn't you?"

"What are you trying to say?" he asked, looking at her.

"You know what I'm saying."

He put his hands on his hips and looked toward Esther and Bennett who were standing a ways behind us. "Them the colored children who've been trespassing on the man's property?"

"Those are the children of Staple Garrison," Grandma said.

"Y'all know catching fish in somebody's pond without permission is stealing?" he asked Esther and Bennett. "Y'all know I could take you both down to the jailhouse right now?"

Neither of them answered. Unflinching and unafraid, they looked into the sheriff's eyes.

He gave a contemptuous snort and looked at Grandma. "Mrs. Grant, I'm just giving these children a warning this time. And that goes for him, too." He nodded at me. "But if I have any more complaints . . ." He didn't finish, knowing she understood.

"I'm going to be at the office of the *Times* first thing in the morning," Grandma said. "I'll take out an ad and tell everybody what you've done."

He smiled and shook his head. "Even if there had been some bones over on Mr. Vorhise's land, nobody has any way of knowing who they belong to."

"What about the belt buckle?" Grandma asked.

"It was right there with the bones," I said. "Esther picked it up right out of the ground."

He took a step closer to me. "Is that right?" he said. I could smell the cigarettes on his breath. "And you saw this? I mean, you with your own eyes saw her reach down into the dirt and pick it up, and you're willing to say that in court?"

I swallowed. Actually, I'd still been up on the hill keeping a look out when she found the buckle. "Bennett saw it," I said. "Bennett saw her pick it up." I nodded in Bennett's direction.

Sheriff Boggs laughed. "Is that so. Well, I hate to have to be the one to tell you this. Your grandmother should have told you. In fact, I think she has a lot to tell you. But the fact of the matter is, he don't count."

I couldn't believe any of this was happening. I felt very light-headed. "But . . . what about Daddy? What about what Daddy saw?"

"What?" he asked.

I looked at Grandma. "Why can't we phone Daddy and ask him? He can tell us whether the man who told him was Mr. Vorhise or not."

Grandma told the sheriff what Daddy had told me on the boat. "Just for drinking out of a dipper," she said as she finished.

The sheriff looked at his watch. "Almost church time. You reckon he'll still be at home?" he asked me.

I cleared my throat. "He don't go to church," I said softly.

Grandma led the way into the house.

We gathered in the hallway as Grandma placed the call.

Mama answered, and Grandma said everything was fine but she needed to speak a minute with Daddy. When Daddy came on the line, she told him someone wanted to talk to him. She handed the phone to the sheriff.

"Hello, Mr. Harrington," Sheriff Boggs said. "We've got a little situation here, and we thought you might help us. Your boy here seems to remember you talking about somebody shooting a colored fellow or something like that. Said he was drinking out of a man's well."

He paused and listened.

After a bit, he smiled and said, "Sure. I know how it is. I got three boys myself." He nodded. "I hate to bother you on a Sunday morning like this." Another pause. "He's right here. You want to talk to him?"

He handed me the phone and I put it to my ear.

"Listen," Daddy said. I could tell he was upset. "I didn't tell you anything like that. You hear me?"

"But Daddy—"

"I mean it, George. I'm telling you this. I said nothing. And that's the way it is. You understand?"

"Yes, sir," I mumbled.

Grandma took the phone from me and hung up.

"He said you probably dreamed it," Sheriff Boggs said to me. "Lots of us get our dreams mixed up with reality. Ain't that so, Mrs. Grant?"

Sheriff Boggs lit a cigarette and blew out the smoke. He looked at Grandma and said, "You can do whatever you think you got to do," he said. "And I got to do what I got to do. And I would advise you very strongly to give all this a lot of thought."

Then he and the deputy left.

Grandma shook her head. "This is absolutely disgusting," she said.

I looked at Esther. She was quaking all over, and every muscle in her body was tense with rage. "I'm gonna kill him!" she said. "I am going to kill that man!"

Thirty-Six

The stream of people going up and down the narrow lane that ran beside Grandma's house to the cabins below was constant throughout the afternoon. It began in full force just after the morning service at Mount Nebo let out.

Two of the deaconesses, dressed in their white church dresses, stood on the porch, welcoming those who came to offer their sympathies. Two other deaconesses stood inside on either side of Elizabeth.

In the tiny kitchen, platters and bowls of food brought by the women quickly covered the counter and table.

Grandma and I had dressed in our Sunday clothes and headed to Elizabeth's. We visited awhile. Elizabeth told Grandma she was hoping somebody could get the word to Winston wherever he was. Then Grandma returned to her house to lie down. She said she felt like she'd been rode hard and put up wet.

Esther and Bennett stood in the room near their mother for a while, but the temperature rose quickly. Outside the house was at least ninety-five degrees in the shade. I have no idea how hot it was in that cabin, but the faces of every person there glistened with sweat.

After Grandma went to take her nap, I sat on the porch, watching the people coming and going on the lane. Esther and Bennett came up in a while and sat on the porch with me. Bennett loosened his tie.

Esther sat in the rocker beside me and looked into my face. "George, I want to know it all," she said. "I want to know everything your daddy told you. Don't leave out a single word."

"It's just what you heard Grandma say."

"No," she said, shaking her head and leaning more toward me. "I want you to start at the beginning. Tell me the whole story."

"Well, it was a Saturday morning, and we were going fishing," I began. I told them about stopping at the restaurant, about the waitress, and how Daddy got upset. I paused for a moment, looking at Bennett. He was staring out toward the chicken house. I could see the rage building up in his eyes.

"Go on," said Esther. "Don't leave out anything."

I told it all, about the storm coming up, about Daddy telling me about the man he knew who had killed a colored man because he was drinking out of his well with the family dipper. "And then the boat turned over," I said. "And when the sheriff asked Daddy about it later, Daddy said I must have dreamed it."

Esther sat back in her chair, put her head against

the back, and rocked gently, slowly. She was looking at the sky and seemed to be thinking. I realized suddenly that what my drunken father told me was probably as much as she and Bennett would learn about what happened to their father. And they knew it.

"Esther," a deep voice said.

We all three turned our heads to look. Reverend Mann had walked up to the edge of the porch without us noticing.

He took off his straw hat and mopped his neck and face with a white handkerchief. He smiled at Esther and said, "May I speak to you for a moment?"

She left with him, and they walked slowly across the yard. He put his hat back on and held his hands behind his back. They walked over toward the barn and stood in the dappled shade of the oak.

Reverend Mann talked. Esther listened with her arms crossed. Occasionally she shook her head, sometimes she nodded, but she never spoke.

In a while, he left and went back toward Elizabeth's, and Esther returned to the porch and sat down.

"What'd he want?" asked Bennett. There was a scowl on his face.

"He says he doesn't want me killing anybody just yet," she said. There was a look in her eyes that I didn't understand, and even though she was sitting, she seemed to be taller. There was something almost glowing about her, just like there had been at the church on Esther Sunday. "He says the time will come when all the Hamans of this world will feel the wrath of God," she continued.

"Who're the Hamans of this world?" I asked.

"The men who always be trying to destroy God's people," she said. "You remember, in the Bible, Esther rises up and saves everyone."

I expected Bennett to make a snort or a wheeze or one of the usual sounds of disgust he makes whenever Esther says something like that. But he didn't.

Instead, in a moment, Bennett said, "I wonder what he did with Daddy's body?"

Esther and Bennett went back to their house. A sleepy calmness had descended upon everything. We had no way of knowing it was the calm, as people say, just before the storm.

In the early evening Bennett returned and said his mother wanted Grandma and me to come eat something, that they had enough food for an army.

We did. Everyone had gone now except an old aunt of Elizabeth's who was dozing in an easy chair. She woke up when we arrived and rose to go. Elizabeth told Bennett to help her down the steps.

After we ate, Grandma sat near Elizabeth, and Elizabeth talked about when she first saw Staple and how they got married. Grandma remembered the wedding.

Then Elizabeth said she thought she'd lie down for a while, and Grandma said she had to go.

Esther, Bennett, and I went outside with her. Darkness was falling.

We walked up the lane. Grandma went back to the house. We walked onto the road and toward town.

Esther talked mostly. She wondered about people in heaven and if they could see what was happening down here, if her father, for example, would ever be able to see her graduate from high school and go to college and get married one day.

"I don't know why you can't send one of your snake friends to see Mr. Vorhise," Bennett grumbled.

Esther laughed softly but didn't reply.

A pickup truck, light colored, maybe white, coming from town, passed us. There were three men sitting in the back of the truck. White men. The truck was driving fast.

I thought of Leroy McInnis, the man who'd beat up Staple.

Esther continued to talk.

Bennett didn't say anything.

We turned around just before we got to the feed store and headed back home.

As we walked on the lane beside Grandma's house, Bennett stopped. "What's that?" he asked.

Down the hill, faintly visible in the moonlight, was something in the lane in front of Elizabeth's cabin. A car? A truck? But who?

There was the sound of a crash, like broken glass, and of men whooping like people do at football games.

Suddenly through the darkness there was an arch of light, of fire, moving from the vehicle to the cabin.

An explosion of fire burst from the cabin.

We stood, like deer transfixed by a spotlight, in the middle of the lane.

I was hardly aware of the light-colored pickup roaring up the hill, spinning its tires, slinging mud, charging toward us. Its lights were on but the truck was hardly visible against the raging fire behind it.

Bennett, like a linebacker, crashed into both me and Esther, and we all plunged into the bramble bushes on the side of the lane. The pickup raced by.

The men in the truck were still whooping.

We scrambled to our feet.

Esther then screamed, "Mama!"

Thirty-Seven

We rushed to the cabin. The entire front was engulfed in flames that snapped, roared, soared into the blackness of the night.

"Around back!" Esther shouted.

Smoke was surging out of the open windows, cascading upwards.

Bennett punched his fist through the screen of Elizabeth's bedroom window, unfastened the hook at the sill, tore off the screen, and flung it behind us.

He scrambled up through the window with Esther and me pushing him. He fell through the window.

I was gagging from the smoke, and my eyes burned.

In a few moments, Elizabeth's head appeared at the window.

"Take her!" Bennett yelled.

Esther and I grabbed hold of her arms and pulled while Bennett pushed from behind. She fell on top of us, and her weight carried us all to the ground.

Bennett came diving out behind her and thudded

to the ground. He groaned and rolled over, holding his left arm.

The roar of the flames got louder. We heard a hissing sound and popping and crashing sounds from within the house.

Esther was up and helped her mother to her feet.

I pushed myself up. Bennett was still on the ground, holding his arm and moaning.

I took him by the shirt and pulled him up. We backed away from the house, which was now a fireball, flames swirling out of every window.

I heard a scream. It was Grandma.

"Over here!" I yelled at her.

The intense heat had driven us back beyond the outhouse. Grandma joined us.

Bennett was bending over, holding his arm and coughing.

Elizabeth sank to the ground, and Esther sat down beside her with her arms around her. Elizabeth leaned forward and began vomiting.

Grandma rushed up, looking from one of us to the other, then to the fire. "I called the fire department," she said. She looked back at us. "Thank God everybody got out."

"Bennett's hurt," I said.

"I think . . . I broke my arm," he said.

I moved around to the other side of Bennett and caught a glimpse of someone moving across the field.

The light of the fire caught the person's movement just for a moment, and then whoever it was, was gone, swallowed up in the night again. I was almost positive it was Auntie Hoosilla.

I heard the siren of the fire truck drawing closer. Other people were rushing about. Reverend Mann and several people from the neighborhood arrived. No one got close to the fire.

In moments, the siren's wail screamed up close, shutting out even the sounds of the fire. The truck bounced down the lane and stopped, and Obadiah's volunteer firemen, wearing yellow helmets and raincoats, yanked hoses off the pumper and hurried about, fighting what was now an inferno.

We backed up farther from the fire as firemen ran around the cabin, shouting back and forth to each other.

They were all excited.

"Listen to me!" barked the short stout man who seemed to be in charge. "Do it right, now. We couldn't have a better practice. Do it right!"

Elizabeth was lying down in the grass. Esther was holding her head in her lap.

Reverend Mann stepped up beside Grandma. "What happened?" he asked.

I quickly told him and Grandma what we'd seen.

"Right now we need to get Elizabeth and Bennett to the hospital," she said.

"Deacon Thompson," Reverend Mann called out to

a man standing in the lane. "We need your car. Go get it and bring it up to the front of Miss Tilly's. We got to get these folks to the hospital."

The man didn't say a word. He turned and started trotting back up the hill.

Reverend Mann looked at me for a moment and then at Grandma. "You know, Miss Tilly, somebody is trying to give somebody a message."

Grandma stood there with her hands on her hips. "You mean someone is sending these children a message? Because of what they found at that pond?"

He nodded gravely. "Yessum," he said. "But I suspect the message isn't just for the children. It's for you as well."

At that moment the house collapsed, and a giant ball of fire rolled up into the dark.

Thirty-Eight

Grandma and I, along with Reverend Mann and Esther, helped Elizabeth up the hill. Bennett followed. Esther got into the backseat of the deacon's car with her mother. Reverend Mann sat up front with the driver.

Grandma phoned Dr. Tatum and told him we needed him to meet us at the clinic right away. She drove her car to town with Bennett in the backseat and me in the front. The deacon followed in his car.

Dr. Tatum was just opening the front door of the clinic when we arrived. He set Bennett's arm—it was broken just above the wrist—and put it into a cast. He examined Elizabeth and said he thought she'd be all right in a few days but ought to stay in bed and rest and drink plenty of fluids.

As everybody was getting back into the cars, Reverend Mann said to Grandma. "We got to find some place they can stay."

"Let's take them to my house," she said. "Tomorrow we'll worry about other arrangements."

Reverend Mann smiled and shook his head as he got back into the deacon's car.

Grandma put Elizabeth in my bed, and said Esther would sleep in the small room on the side that used to be Matthew's. She made pallets on the floor in the front room for me and Bennett.

She then told me to go back to the fire and find out what was going on. And to be careful. She and Esther were going to change Elizabeth's clothes and put her to bed. Bennett stretched out on his pallet. He felt a little dizzy.

All was dark at Elizabeth's. The fire truck and everyone were gone. I shined the flashlight around the smoldering piles of rubble. Only the chimney and the brick piers on which the house stood were still standing.

I returned home, bathed, and got ready for bed. Bennett and Esther both had had to dress in some of my underthings. Grandma gave Esther one of her gowns to wear as well. It was after midnight.

In the morning, Reverend Mann was at the house early. He'd already rounded up some clothes for Esther, Bennett, and Elizabeth.

Grandma didn't open the store. We all went down to the remains of the cabin, except for Elizabeth, of course. She stayed in bed.

Grandma shook her head as we walked down. "She just keeps saying, 'All my pictures gone. All my pictures gone.'"

We used rakes and shovels to work through the ashes. Wisps of smoke still rose in a few places.

The house only had four rooms—the front room, two bedrooms, and the kitchen. The kitchen was barely bigger than a closet.

The iron stove lay on its side where the kitchen had been. Esther was hard at work going through the room she had shared with her mother. She told me to work through the front room. Bennett, with his one good arm, could do what he could, she said, but was not to overdo it. Grandma was working in the other bedroom, the one Bennett and Winston had shared up until Winston left a few weeks ago.

The sun was already hot by eight o'clock. Reverend Mann came back about ten o'clock with a carton of cold Cokes. "I had to get these in town," he said apologetically to Grandma, "since you ain't open yet."

Grandma, Bennett, me, and Reverend Mann sat in the shade of the sweet gum on the other side of the lane and drank our soda pops. The leaves of the tree were withered and scorched by the heat. Esther continued to work. "I'll drink it later," she told Reverend Mann.

"Now Miss Tilly," the pastor said, "we need to start thinking of where we're going to put these folks. Everybody at the church is pretty crowded, but we've already had several offers. Of course, I was wondering about that place down there." He nodded toward the vacant cabin not far away.

Bennett drank deeply and acted like he wasn't listening. Of course, I knew he was.

Grandma looked down at the drink she was holding in her lap. Then she looked at me as if waiting for me to make a suggestion.

"Why can't they just stay with us?" I asked.

Grandma grinned and looked back at Reverend Mann. "That sounds like the easiest solution," she said. "Besides, ain't no sense in trying to move Elizabeth just yet."

Reverend Mann frowned. "You can't be serious, Miss Tilly. That would put not only you and your grandson in danger, but Elizabeth and these children as well. They could make one big fire out of that house of yours."

Grandma took a long swallow of her drink and looked at me again. "What do you think?"

I grinned at her. "If they burn the house, we'll just all move into that cabin," I said.

She nodded at the minister. "Sounds good to me, Reverend," she said.

"Yippee!" yelled Esther. "I found it!"

We all turned to look at her. She was grinning and walking though the blackened rumble toward us, and she held up something in her fingers. As she drew closer, I could see it was a silver dog's-head belt buckle.

Thirty-Nine

On Tuesday, Grandma reopened the store. Since Elizabeth was still resting at home, Esther handled the kitchen by herself with some help from Grandma. Bennett went to take care of the cows.

Grandma told him that since he was going into the eighth grade and would graduate next May, maybe then he would like to run the farm for her. Her father, she said, had run a farm by himself at fourteen, and she couldn't see any reason why he couldn't. She said she'd get another farmer to help out until he finished the year.

By Wednesday the entire community of Obadiah was shocked and scandalized by the fact that the Garrisons were living under the same roof with us. The blacks were shocked, and the whites were scandalized. It was as if their collective breath had been knocked out of them and they were still too dizzy to respond.

At the midweek prayer meeting at the Obadiah Methodist Church, Grandma stood up to testify. She gave praises to God that no one was hurt in the fire that had destroyed her tenant house. She asked that they not think she was putting on airs once they heard that she had done what many of the best families in Montgomery were doing, namely, hiring "live-in help."

Two rows in front of us, Mrs. Crampton, wife of Mr. Otis Crampton, the richest man in Obadiah, jabbed her husband in the side with her elbow. I figured by tomorrow noon Mrs. Crampton would be hiring live-in help also.

Thursday morning we were all sitting around the table at breakfast. Elizabeth was fully dressed and said she felt strong enough to go back to work. At least, she said, she'd do as much as she could.

Esther said she sure didn't want to have some crazy Haman burn Grandma's house down on top of our heads, that there simply wasn't room for everybody in that falling down vacant cabin down the lane, and she had a suggestion.

"When I'm working at Mrs. York's, I'm supposed to answer the phone by saying, 'York residence.' I think that's what we ought to do here." She looked from her mother to Bennett. "We ought to all answer the phone by saying, 'Grant residence.'"

Esther also told us that the plans were set for Reverend Mann to funeralize Staple Saturday morning at 10:30 at Mount Nebo. There would be a dinner-on-the-grounds after the service.

Grandma stood up and carried some dishes to the sink just as the telephone rang. She stepped into the hallway to answer it.

"Hel—" She stopped herself and looked back at us and grinned. "Grant residence," she said.

Bennett started laughing, then Esther, then me and Elizabeth. We laughed until we cried.

On Friday, Sheriff Boggs came to talk to Grandma. He said Mr. Vorhise had gotten an anonymous phone call. Mr. Vorhise said it sounded like a disguised voice. He wasn't sure whether it was a man or woman, and this caller said Mr. Vorhise was going to get bitten by a cottonmouth. Maybe the snake would be in a sack of dog food, maybe in his pickup, maybe in his bed.

Grandma said that would be a terrible thing to have to live with every day, worrying about something like that, and, no, she had no idea who would make such a call.

At the funeral service Saturday Reverend Mann said, "Deacon Staple Garrison was a godly man who took care of his family. He was not one of these men who run off somewheres and don't feed their little ones. He loved his wife and children, and he did everything a man is supposed to do."

"Amen!" said several people.

He went on to say that somebody had asked him if he thought the mortal remains of Deacon Staple Garrison would ever be found. "I told that man—yes,

I did—I told that man, the bones of Brother Staple may be lost, but Brother Staple himself was not lost. He was found by the Great Shepherd of the sheep himself and—this is what I told him—he is resting right at this very moment in the bosom of Jesus!"

"Yes, he is!" several shouted all at once.

"And while the person that stole his earthly life may not be behind iron bars—and probably never will be—that one bears the mark of Cain. And wherever he walks in this community, folks going to look at him and know he spilled innocent blood. Whenever that man looks another person in the face around here, he'll wonder if that person is thinking he's a killer."

There was a nodding of assent around the church house.

After the service we ate on the tables nailed up between the trees at the back of the church. When we were done, we sat in Grandma's car, ready to go. Grandma stayed behind to talk a moment with Reverend Mann.

Esther, Bennett, and Elizabeth were sitting in the backseat, and I was in the front. The heat was stifling.

"Sister Tupper said how pretty you looked in that dress," Elizabeth said to Esther.

Esther sighed. "It was her daughter's."

Elizabeth smiled and said, "I know. But I still thought it was nice of her to say so."

Esther closed her eyes a moment and said very slowly, "One day . . . and I mean this with all my heart . . . one day I ain't living a hand-me-down life."

Grandma opened her door and got in. "Ready?" she asked.

When we got out of the car at Grandma's house and were going inside Grandma pulled me to one side and asked, "Are you sure about this?"

I nodded my head, "Yes, ma'am," I said.

I was sure, but I wanted to get it over and done with. I didn't know why I had to do it. I just knew I did. Sometimes you just have to do the things you know you have to without really knowing why.

Grandma told Bennett she'd feel a lot more easy knowing the cows were all right. Did he feel up to checking on them? He changed clothes and shoes and left.

Grandma asked Esther if she would mind walking down to Aunt Glendora and Aunt Olivia's, that in all the hurly-burly of the last few days she hadn't been able to look in on them at all, and they could both have left the country, for all she knew. "I'd send George, but I need him to do something else for me."

Esther looked surprised at the request, but left immediately.

With both of them out of the house, Grandma asked Elizabeth to please sit down at the table in the kitchen. Grandma and I sat down at the table also. Elizabeth looked puzzled.

Grandma was holding a thick envelope in her hands.

"Elizabeth, someone—and I am not at liberty to say who—feels very strongly that Esther needs to go on to Adamstown to the high school there this next year. In this envelope is one hundred dollars."

One hundred dollars? But I had given Grandma only sixty-six dollars. That meant Grandma must have given thirty-four dollars of her own money.

"This morning before the service, Reverend Mann talked on the phone with the lady at the high school in Adamstown," continued Grandma. "She is looking forward to Esther coming next Wednesday to register for school."

Elizabeth looked too stunned to speak.

"And for goodness sake, Elizabeth. Tell her it ain't charity. It's an investment. Yes, that's what it is. An investment."

Grandma told Elizabeth that she ought to go lie down, that she and I were going on down to open the store for a couple of hours in case somebody needed something before suppertime.

As I entered the store I thought about this being my last working day. Tomorrow was Sunday, and in the afternoon Grandma was driving me back home to Mobile. Monday I would register for the eighth grade.

I stood just inside the front door and looked around at the store.

Grandma walked behind the cash register, then turned her face to me and smiled. It was like she was reading my mind. "I'll miss you," she said. "And all you have to do is pick up the phone and call. I can be down there quicker than a tick can jump on a hound's back. You know that." The register clanged as she opened the cash drawer. "And your mother and I have already talked," she continued. "You just think about it."

I nodded and took the feather duster and began working on the cans of green peas. It wasn't something I wanted to think about right then.

I looked out through the front window into the outside glare and almost fell against the shelves. I couldn't believe my eyes. Coming across the street toward the store through the bright haze, drawing ever closer and closer, was Auntie Hoosilla.

She shuffled on, her hood drawn down over her face, and in her hand she held a leash. On the leash was a dog. Not just any dog, but my dog. Dog! And Dog was wearing a pink bow.

"Grandma!" I said rushing over to the counter. "Look! Auntie Hoosilla . . . and she stole Dog!"

"Auntie Drusilla," corrected Grandma, "and she didn't steal your dog."

"But . . ."

"In her way of thinking she paid for that dog. Now, hush up. We'll talk about it later."

Out front, Auntie Drusilla bent down slowly and tied the leash to the bottom of one of the porch posts. Then she came inside. Her black snap purse hung from her arm.

"Good afternoon, Auntie Drusilla," Grandma said cheerily. "Can we help you today?"

Grandma took a basket and walked around the counter. "I know you'll want some soup today," she said, picking up a can of Campbell's. "Tomato all right?"

The old woman nodded.

"And George if you would kindly go get the snuff. Three dots, remember."

I got the snuff and brought it to the basket. I wasn't happy about this situation at all. Grandma had a lot of explaining to do as far as I was concerned.

When she had all of the things she wanted in the basket, Auntie Drusilla stepped closer to the counter and opened her purse. She reached inside and carefully brought out a flower, an angel flower, and laid it on the counter.

Then she withdrew another, and another, until she had seven angel flowers lined up on the counter all in a row.

"They're lovely, Auntie," Grandma said. "Let me put this all in a bag for you."

I stalked to the front window and looked out at Dog lying in the shade beside the post. I couldn't believe it. My dog was wearing some dumb pink bow, and my grandmother was selling groceries for weeds.

I turned to look back at them, and my breath went out of me as surely as if somebody had kicked me in the pit of my stomach.

Auntie Drusilla Cardamone was reaching up her

hand to Grandma's face. Now she was touching it gently, patting the side of her face.

Grandma brought up both of her hands to Auntie Drusilla's hood and pushed it back a little.

I'd never seen anything so horrible in all my life. Her head was bald, exactly like Bennett had been told. Shaggy patches of hair grew in spots, but mostly she was bald.

She had no eyebrows, and her nose looked like it had been eaten away. Her head and face were covered with crinkled, discolored skin of several colors— brown, white, and red.

Grandma ran her hands tenderly over Auntie Drusilla's face, then leaned forward and kissed her on the cheek.

Auntie Drusilla was smiling—if you can call what that twisted mouth was doing a smile—and then she picked up the bag and shuffled my way.

As she passed me she looked up at me. One eye was missing. Gone. There was nothing there. She was still smiling.

She went out the door and set the bag down, untied Dog, picked up the bag again, and walked out into the bright afternoon glare.

Suddenly I knew. I understood. I knew exactly what that crinkled, discolored skin was. It was massive scar tissue folded all across her head and face, old scar tissue, the exact kind of scar tissue that someone would have who, many, many years ago, had rushed into a burning house and rushed out again with something very precious wrapped in a blanket.

I turned around to look at Grandma. She was smiling and crying. I turned to look out the front window again. Auntie Drusilla and Dog were already gone.

In addition to being a husband, father, and grand-father, John Armistead is religion editor of the *Northeast Mississippi Daily Journal,* has taught kindergarten and high school, and served as pastor of various churches for twenty-five years. He has published three novels, *A Legacy of Vengeance, A Homecoming for Murder,* and *Cruel as the Grave.* He is also a painter and has exhibited in shows and festivals throughout the South. Armistead's favorite hobby is his Harley-Davidson. He lives in Mississippi.

If you enjoyed this book, you'll also want to read these other Milkweed novels.

To order books or for more information, contact Milkweed at (800) 520-6455 or visit our website (www.milkweed.org).

Gildaen, The Heroic Adventures of a Most Unusual Rabbit
by Emilie Buchwald

Chicago Tribune Book Festival Award,
Best Book for Ages 9–12

Gildaen is befriended by a mysterious being who has lost his memory but not the ability to change shape at will. Together they accept the perilous task of thwarting the evil sorcerer, Grimald, in this tale of magic, villainy, and heroism.

The Ocean Within
by V. M. Caldwell

Milkweed Prize for Children's Literature

Elizabeth is a foster child who has just been placed with the boisterous and affectionate Sheridans, a family that wants to adopt her. Used to having to look out for herself, however, Elizabeth is reluctant to open up to them. During a summer spent by the ocean with the eight Sheridan children and their grandmother, who Elizabeth dubs "Iron Woman" because of her strict discipline, Elizabeth learns what it means—and how much she must risk—to become a permanent member of a loving family.

No Place
by Kay Haugaard

Arturo Morales and his fellow sixth-grade classmates decide to improve their neighborhood and their lives by building a park in their otherwise concrete, inner-city Los Angeles barrio. The kids are challenged by their teachers to figure out what it would take to transform the neighborhood junkyard into a clean, safe place for children to play. Despite their parents' skepticism and the threat of street gangs, Arturo and his classmates struggle to prove that the actions of individuals—even kids—can make a difference.

Business As Usual
by David Haynes

from the West 7th Wildcats Series

In Mr. Harrison's sixth-grade class, the West 7th Wildcats must learn how to run a business. Kevin Olsen, one of the Wildcats as well as the class clown, is forced out of the Wildcat group and into an unwilling alliance working in a group with the Wildcats' nemesis, Jenny Pederson. In the process of making staggering amounts of cookies for Marketplace Day, the classmates venture into the realm of free enterprise, discovering more than they imagined about business, the world, and themselves.

The Gumma Wars
by David Haynes

from the West 7th Wildcats Series

Larry "Lu" Underwood and his fellow West 7th Wildcats have been looking forward to Tony Rodriguez's birthday fiesta all year—only to discover that Lu must also spend the day with his two feuding "gummas," the name he gave his grandmothers when he was just learning to talk. The two "gummas," Gumma Jackson and Gumma Underwood, are hostile to one another, especially when it comes to claiming the affection of their only grandson. On the action-packed day of Tony's birthday, Lu, a friend, and the gummas find themselves exploring the sights of Minneapolis and St. Paul—and eventually find themselves enjoying each other's company.

The Monkey Thief
by Aileen Kilgore Henderson

New York Public Library Best Books of the Year: "Books for the Teen Age"

Twelve-year-old Steve Hanson is sent to Costa Rica for eight months to live with his uncle. There he discovers a world completely unlike anything he can see from the cushions of his couch back home, a world filled with giant trees and insects, mysterious sounds, and the constant companionship of monkeys swinging in the branches overhead. When Steve hatches a plan to capture a monkey for himself, his quest for a pet leads him into dangerous territory. It takes all of Steve's survival skills—and the help of his new friends—to get him out of trouble.

The Summer of the Bonepile Monster
by Aileen Kilgore Henderson

Milkweed Prize for Children's Literature

Alabama Library Association 1996 Juvenile/ Young Adult Award

Eleven-year-old Hollis Orr has been sent to spend the summer with Grancy, his father's grandmother, in rural Dolliver, Alabama, while his parents "work things out." As summer begins, Hollis encounters a road called Bonepile Hollow, barred by a gate and a real skull and bones mounted on a board. "Things that go down that road don't ever come back," he is told. Thus begins the mystery that plunges Hollis into real danger.

Treasure of Panther Peak
by Aileen Kilgore Henderson

Twelve-year-old Page Williams begrudgingly accompanies her mother, Ellie, as she flees her abusive husband, Page's father. Together they settle in a fantastic new world—Big Bend National Park, Texas. Wild animals stalk through the park, and the nearby Ghost Mountains are filled with legends of lost treasures. As Page tests her limits by sneaking into forbidden canyons, Ellic struggles to win the trust of other parents. Only through their newfound courage are they able to discover a treasure beyond what they could have imagined.

I Am Lavina Cumming
by Susan Lowell

Mountains & Plains Booksellers Association Award

In 1905, ten-year-old Lavina is sent from her home on the Bosque Ranch in Arizona Territory to live with her aunt in the city of Santa Cruz, California. Armed with the Cumming family motto, "courage," Lavina deals with a new school, homesickness, a very spoiled cousin, an earthquake, and a big decision about her future.

The Boy with Paper Wings
by Susan Lowell

Confined to bed with a viral fever, eleven-year-old Paul sails a paper airplane into his closet and propels himself into mysterious and dangerous realms in this exciting and fantastical adventure. Paul finds himself trapped in the military diorama on his closet floor, out to stop the evil commander, KRON. Armed only with paper and the knowledge of how to fold it, Paul uses his imagination and courage to find his way out of dilemmas and disasters.

The Secret of the Ruby Ring
by Yvonne MacGrory

Winner of Ireland's Bisto "Book of the Year" Award

Lucy gets a very special birthday present, a star ruby ring, from her grandmother and finds herself transported to Langley Castle in the Ireland of 1885. At first, she is intrigued by castle life, in which she is the lowliest servant, until she loses the ruby ring and her only way home.

A Bride for Anna's Papa
by Isabel R. Marvin

Milkweed Prize for Children's Literature

Life on Minnesota's iron range in 1907 is not easy for thirteen-year-old Anna Kallio. Her mother's death has left Anna to take care of the house, her young brother, and her father, a blacksmith in the dangerous iron mines. So she and her brother plot to find their father a new wife, even attempting to arrange a match with one of the "mail order" brides arriving from Finland.

Minnie
by Annie M. G. Schmidt

Winner of the Netherlands' Silver Pencil Prize as One of the Best Books of the Year

Miss Minnie is a cat. Or rather, she *was* a cat. She is now a human, and she's not at all happy to be one. As Minnie tries to find and reverse the cause of her transformation, she brings her reporter friend, Mr. Tibbs, news from the cats' gossip hotline—including revealing information that one of the town's most prominent citizens is not the animal lover he appears to be.

The Dog with Golden Eyes
by Frances Wilbur

Milkweed Prize for Children's Literature

Many girls dream of owning a dog of their own, but Cassie's wish for one takes an unexpected turn in this contemporary tale of friendship and growing up. Thirteen-year-old Cassie is lonely, bored, and feeling friendless when a large, beautiful dog appears one day in her suburban backyard. Cassie wants to adopt the dog, but as she learns more about him, she realizes that she is, in fact, caring for a full-grown Arctic wolf. As she attempts to protect the wolf from urban dangers, Cassie discovers that she possesses strengths and resources she never imagined.

Behind the Bedroom Wall
by Laura E. Williams

Milkweed Prize for Children's Literature

New York Public Library Best Books of the Year: "Books for the Teen Age"

It is 1942. Thirteen-year-old Korinna Rehme is an active member of her local *Jungmädel*, a Nazi youth group, along with many of her friends. Korinna's parents, however, secretly are members of an underground group providing a means of escape to the Jews of their city and are, in fact, hiding a refugee family behind the wall of Korinna's bedroom. As Korinna comes to know the family, and their young daughter, her sympathies begin to turn. But when someone tips off the Gestapo, loyalties are put to the test and Korinna must decide in what she believes and whom she trusts.

The Spider's Web
by Laura E. Williams

Thirteen-year-old Lexi Jordan has just joined The Pack, a group of neo-Nazi skinheads, as a substitute for the family she wishes she had. After she and The Pack spray paint a synagogue, Lexi hides from her pursuers on the front porch of elderly Ursula Zeidler, a former member of the Hitler Youth Group, who painfully recalls her ugly anti-Semitic Nazi activities and betrayal of a friend that she bitterly rues. When her younger sister becomes enthralled with Lexi's new "family," Lexi realizes the true meaning of The Pack and has little time to save herself and her sister from its sinister grip.

Interior design by Wendy Holdman
Typeset in Charlotte Book and Mister Earl
by Stanton Publication Services, Inc.
Printed on acid-free 55 # Sebago Antique Cream paper
by Maple-Vail Book Manufacturing

DATE DUE

#47-0108 Peel Off Pressure Sensitive